HANDICAP THIS

A Disabled Life Guide

THOMAS WHITNEY

Fulton Books, Inc.
Meadville, PA

Published by Fulton Books 2021

ISBN 978-1-63710-302-9 (paperback)
ISBN 978-1-63710-326-5 (hardcover)
ISBN 978-1-63710-303-6 (digital)

Printed in the United States of America

even seen the people who spend so much time in mediocrity, and the footprint left is just inside another. Then sometimes, just sometimes (okay, this is probably most of us), there are those who have the "bite your lip, bend over, and take it with no lube" type of life. If this type of life is bothersome or the vulgarity of the bold, basic truth is not your style, then stop reading right here because this is not your reading material.

The basis behind my writing comes from my life experience, and no amount of motivational material can help that. You will come along on the journey of learning life lessons with me through my dark humor and handicapped life. Here, I will give you my uneasy topics, which you have to learn to live and deal with. Life will hit you straight in the face—think of a boxer learning to bruise; that is the purpose here. The story is not for the faint of heart and is not meant for all audiences. I have encountered quite a few things in my short time here on earth. While I understand there are plenty who have it far worse (for that I am sorry), and there are plenty that have it far better (kindly piss off. Sincerely, the average person). These are my prerequisites to have you continue perusing this depiction of life with me.

However, if this sounds like it might relate to your kind of life or sound like something that may just tickle your fancy, read on. I promise you three things: First, you will be offended either by the horrible story/life lessons or the verbiage I spew

Life is one perplexing experience and ordeal. Behind its intangibility, mystery, and diversity, humanity never gets the deep meaning. It is a meaning that lacks a concrete and tangible answer that further compounds its purpose. However, despite everything—the chaos, mystery, and hullaballoo—life goes on! Whether one is silly, weird, happy, sad, or whatever, it goes on. It is a tragic reality to wake up to the same problems of yesterday. Things go on; they happen as humans get busy converting oxygen into carbon dioxide. It reaches a point in life when the brain goes like, "I shouldn't do that" to "What the heck, get over it, dude, and see the changes." Life is one funny hell of an experience. Despite its absurdity, confusion, chaos, downs, it is all about the experience—the good, the bad, the ugly, the shitty, and all the nonsense put into one breath!

Life…has a funny way of really reaching us all. Some people have the perfect, happy, sunshine-on-their-shoulders type of life. Some people have the "put your head down, work hard, and everything will be all right" type of life. Hell, I have

This book is dedicated to my friends, my family, and a few writers that have helped me along the way. All of you will remain nameless to spare any annoyance this may cause, which it will, so *love you*!

A special thank-you to my father. I hope that one day, if I ever really grow up, I can be half the man that you are. You mean the world to all of us, Pop.

To my fiancée, ha ha, sucker. You said yes. I hope everyone that knows you says sorry, as you are stuck with my twisted ass! Thank you for all the love and support along the journey of life.

hereafter. Second, I speak the harsh reality of life that the majority of the not-top percent of society will understand. Lastly, life, much like the spatter of boiling water when you add the pasta, burns us all. Well, you have made it this far with me, so enjoy the read, and if you feel me… I understand and I am sorry.

WHAT A NOVEL START

Our story begins in a quiet little town in Central New York in the mid-1980s. To set the mood, you need to understand depiction and actuality. Many people hear New York and instantly think New York City, the Big Apple—ask the exchange students, foreigners, or anyone south of New York never traveling there. Rural Central New York is very quiet, with vast hills, beautiful foliage, and the faint sound of "agricultural" noises off in the distances. Sounds real nice right, does it not? To most people in a metropolitan area, this is the dream you read about. In fact, we are taught everywhere that this is the illustration of the happily ever after. The proverbial place you would find the big farmhouse with the five bedrooms, wood stove, garden, large yard, and the white picket fence. Now that, folks, is the average illustration of what this small rural countryside is expected to be. We read about this in many books as children, shows portray this on television, and our parents at least my generation tell us this is what we should aim for. You get told from the start of your young life you will grow up be strong, go to school, get a degree, get a great job, get married, move to the country, and thus obtain said dream mentioned above. This is what we are molded to believe and made to think is the way it goes. This is the depiction or representation of this area and life that people want you to know and understand. Seriously, I would be willing to bet that 90 percent of you reading or listening to this are saying, "Yeah, I definitely can relate to this so far, sounds exactly like what I was told and am now working toward." The projected depiction of what our lives are said to be…it is a complex dream that we set ourselves up for.

Actuality is defined as "actual existence typically as contrasted with what was intended, believed, or expected." Let me be the first to tell you actuality hits you straight in the face, and it hits like the well-packed snowball from the bully at school. The giant dream and illustration you have of what life is and is going to be is just wrong. Rural Central New York, could it have all those things depicted in the illusion of our childhood brainwashing, you say? Well, of course, it can, but could a beautiful blue ocean have dangers? The actuality of what the area is that it is full of hard-working blue-collar families struggling to face worldly strife. The land is mostly underdeveloped and what is not is farmed. That house with the white picket fence is damaged and is caving in on itself from the years of neglect. The air smells of freshly spread manure, and the scent from freshly harvested crop causes more allergic reaction than smiles. It is tough living in this dream area. Farmers work countless hours to produce milk, feed, crops, and items we buy for $2.99 at the grocery store. Sixteen-hour days to get a price for grain and milk that barely keeps the lights on. This just to go home and work on that dream mansion farmhouse that we idolize in our fantasy as the ideal place to live with our five kids, dog, and wife. The harsh truth of life is that it is not what it seems. We hear the grass is greener on the other side; is it or is it really just the same color green we associate with sick? In many of these areas I speak of, it's twenty minutes just to get to something that resembles a department store or a large market store. So I ask, does it really sound like the wonderful dream we are trained to believe?

The first life lesson hits hard when you figure it out. Perception is not always reality, and this is the first thing we must learn. We perceive all these things to be true because our parents, schoolteachers and stories told us so. Truth in life is sometimes a funny thing. The way of life either in metropolitan areas or rural areas is far different than what we are told. In the "big cities," the high-rise living with the hustle and bustle looks great in Hollywood and stories. The same can be said for the "country life." It is interesting the slate of lies we begin with and grow up looking forward to as an endgame. This idea of life gives us purpose, a pathway to grow ourselves, and a reason to strive toward that goal of success. What we need to understand is this also gives us unreal expectations, most times, dismal chances to achieve, and, worst of all, leaves us unprepared for the circumstances that everyday life will throw at you.

Now I am sure by this point you are thinking, *Well, this guy sure can bitch.* You are right, I sure can. But tell me, am I wrong? I challenge you to think about this, and if you have faced, heard, or dealt with any of the above, *you* know exactly what I am saying. Perceptions and depictions of what our life is supposed to be rule our lives. They govern over us like some kind of warden or sheriff, crippling our actual monotonous daily lives. Learning this lesson in life is usually done the hard way unfortunately, and it is needed for us to continue to give up on the small strife of our routines. The understanding now portrayed of the depiction of what it is meant to be and the actuality of what is real most certainly is crucial to life. It is meant more for a worldly view, not just what I described. Now I understand that the long-winded description I gave you may seem over the top, but it is real, and the sooner you figure that out in your own life, the more you will be able to move on from the unsurmountable weight that holds you back. We as humans strive to obtain all these things to the point where these perceptions of the ideal life drive us mad. While I am a common person and may not be able to give scientific proof here, look at the mental health state of your own area. I would be willing to be the results are not well, and life pressures cause that. This causes you to make choices, and those choices cause so many issues in our lives. I cannot tell you how to overcome these hurdles, and those motivational people who tell you they have the answer are just wrong. It is not how we fall; everyone falls, believe that. Once you fall, you must rise, and there it lies. It does *lie*; perceptions ingrained into us make the rise so hard. I am telling you, it does not have to be quite so hard; you can adapt to an easier way to make the wheel roll along. I will take you along my journey and help you find what I found. We each must find our own path and not worry about perceptions others lay out for us. Let that sink in; it is a hard pill to swallow. No deep breaths, meditation, or miracle preacher's water is going to fix that. As soon as you realize that you are the answer, the sooner you can sit down and eat your ice cream in peace.

CHAPTER 2

ROCKY ROAD ISN'T JUST ICE CREAM

Rocky road is not just an ice cream flavor—and that might just be the truest statement you will ever read. Sometimes in life, there are bumps in the road that you must encounter in order to become who you are. How many times have you heard that from an important figure in your life? I would argue this might be the biggest understatement you encounter in a lifetime. We all have something we feel is the biggest influence and/or hurdle we have overcome, sometimes without us even knowing this may be one of the most crucial points in our life. This dish is almost always served cold from the strong fist of the universe.

Everyone's moment is different; the problems and hurdles of life that shape who we are, different. However, the similarity is the fact we all face them at some point. The biggest event in my life was at the very beginning, at a ripe old age of three weeks. At this stage, everyone is so excited to just be alive because we know no better. An infant holds the key to true happiness, and that is pure unindulged ignorance of the forthcoming train wreck. At this age, who thinks something so dramatic could happen it changes your life? Immediately from the outside, you stare puzzled, pondering this statement. I would hope nothing is the answer you are thinking, and most times, this early in life, that holds true. However, it is that one rare instance I mentioned earlier that can quickly change your reality and mold you.

In that small rural area I spoke of is where I learned this harsh lesson. My mother and father were headed from a shopping center to return home. However, we lived in another even more rural area several miles from the shopping centers, thus causing travel across a large portion of less densely populated section to get to a strip mall. On the commute home, my parents encountered a motorist who should not have been on the road. This driver had been at the local watering hole and had several drinks, got up, went to his car, and left for home. On his travels, he left the rural watering hole and headed through that less dense area back to his house. As my parents traveled that road on that faithful night in October, the two vehicles crossed paths. I do mean crossed quite literally; this gentleman crossed the highway and struck my parents head on. This led to a horrific crash that nearly took my mother's life and severely injured my father. After a long rehabilitation and several close calls, they told my mother she would survive but forever be paralyzed. The likelihood of surviving the injuries she sustained especially at that time was not thought possible. The list of things for people handicapped to her extent at that time was slim to nonexistent. How? Oh Lord, how could the universe do this to these newlyweds and brand-new parents?

Freeze it here, this moment right in time, not caused by my family or myself. The universe had taught me a lesson before I even had a chance to get started. That lesson was life's a bitch, but we deal with it and move on. The rocky road was not a sweet treat that you could overindulge and have an upset tummy. However, for the rest of my life, it has upset my stomach, my pride, my daily living, and my attitude without even knowing it for a very long time. I myself had the blissful ignorance of an infant and still had no care in the world at that time.

So we move on and into how this lesson makes life something of a tangled web we must overcome. Well, this, as one would imagine, made things very interesting in my life. We as a family had to learn to work through the trials and tribulations that life throws our way. Not every life has such a quick incident that teaches them this lesson. You all will have that moment you understand that life's a bitch and you deal with it. I mean, seriously, how many times have you heard that all over the place? Maybe you were at work, maybe you were at school, maybe from your parents; hell, maybe it has not even happened yet. Rest assured, you will encounter this moment, and it is of the utmost importance that you pay attention to it. If you listen when it strikes and you lick your wounds and move on, it will help you through times you could not even imagine.

The importance here in life lays right within your own imprisoned imagination. This moment will hit, and when it does, how will you be able to handle it? Confined in our own consciousness is the key to strength beyond your wildest beliefs. We all have the will power to overcome the craziest things we may encounter. The trick is, we can harness that. For me, personally, it happened so young, the ignorance of youth covered the fear and indifference. I did not know any better, so I did not think any better. Fucked from the start without knowing you are fucked really puts a different spin on it.

The uncomfortable truth that you must face in the moment (when it happens) is how do we move on, what is left to give me a reason to move on. Hope is not the answer you seek. First, understanding that hope is not a necessity and, in fact, weighs you down is crucial. Hope is a mislabeled portion of life that we have trapped in our mind. The sad truth is hope is fucked itself. Hope sets us up for failure, hope makes us always think something is better or worse. Hope deceives us continually into caring about opinions instead of ourselves. Do not close the book and get pissed now; we are just getting started. I am not saying there is no reason to go forward, and there is no reason to continue. I am saying if you base your life on hope… Life's a bitch, and you will not make it. You will hope everything perfect, and then life will happen much like a Mack Truck encounters a Prius in a highway collision.

Insanity is defined as doing the same thing repeatedly and expecting a different result. So if you continue to hope everything will get better, hope for a brighter future, and hope that tomorrow will be better, all is well, right? What happens when hope gets you shit? This is what I am saying—tomorrow does not get better if you do not make it better. The future is yours to mold, and things are what you make them. I could have easily rolled over when I got old enough to realize that not only was my mother paralyzed but our life would forever be crippled by the medical bills and constant struggle. The stress of that life is enough to make anyone break, believe me. You know what did not fix everything? Yup, you guessed it—hope. There was no hope my mother would walk, there was no hope for relief from medical bills, and there was no hope it would be different tomorrow. Do you wake up in the morning and hope you have a coffee? No, we get up and make our coffee or use our hard-earned money to buy a coffee; hope does not handle that for us. Hope that self-centered bastard gets us hyped just to drop off over the edge.

Internally, hope destroys us slowly, by never living up to the expectations set forth. Well, simply put, fuck that. Are you going to let someone else's false pretenses that have been instilled in us dictate our own needs? So, from here on out, say it with me: "Fuck hope." It is motivation you need, nothing more! Motivation is the drive to get through that "life's a bitch, we move on" moment(s). Okay, so now you ask how the hell do we get motivated without hope? Well, guess what you *do not* need—hope. Remember me telling you hope weighs you down, and makes you focus on perceptions, et cetera. I am going to address that notion right now with a question for you to think about. Does hope make things happen or do you make things happen? You make things happen! If something happens to your car and you cannot get to work, do you hope your car gets fixed? What makes you get it fixed, life needs to happen, and you have to get it fixed to continue on should be what you are thinking here. Hope is not going to fix your catalytic converter just like it will not fix your mental flow.

Now motivation is the key to getting the car of life going. Let me tell you that is the real trick to progression—finding that motivation to go on. One thing to keep in mind as you find your own path: it is not the perception of what people dream about for you. You may want to be rich; motivation for you is money then. Surely you can hope for money, likely just as the dream that is the depiction of the "perfect home front" from earlier, although it is probably not going to just happen. If you put your head down, work hard, and really push, you can obtain it, but hope is not going to make that happen—you are. Maybe money is not your success story; maybe you drive comes from family. Hope does not make family happen or grow. However, you can go out and find the right person to work at that with. My point here is that *hoping* to have what is this fantasy of the perfect life is a farce. Chasing the fairy tale that is embedded in your head only leads to failure.

The very first thing you need to do is understand what *you* want. Now hell, that sounds pretty easy, right? It took me twenty-five years to figure that out. I was chasing expectations and dreams that were pushed on me by television, teachers, and family. It hit me like a ton of bricks all the sudden one day. I was talking with my now fiancée who told me I was miserable and needed an attitude adjustment. I worked eighty plus hours a week, had a decent amount of money, a decent set of jobs, and her, so I thought I was doing well. After a few rough conversations about my attitude and falling asleep sitting in an armchair, it dawned on me. I worked myself miserable trying to appease the norm. All I really had was a bad attitude, a bank account, and a long workweek which, in turn, was driving my other half nuts.

Self-reflection is a key tool to help you find the motivation to navigate through the dense forest of life. I realized working my life away to get a house with the picket fence and monetary wealth was not everything that mattered. Understanding your own goals—not anyone else's—is the path you need to find. I would love to tell you it is exactly this and that is the key. Sure, I would like *the* ideal place to call home and the whole nine yards, but was it worth sacrificing your whole damn life to get there? The sooner that you realize it is not all glitter and gold, the more empowered you will be.

It is funny how we as a society put such a take on what is and how we get there. We spend all our lives focused on this idealization of perfect. The perfect body, the perfect health, the perfect house, the perfect partner, equaling the perfect life. Perfect, perfect, perfect. But does it really mean anything? What good is perfect in the vision of *your* future? Is it what that image is that is painted out for you? As soon as you use self-reflection as a tool, you will realize what actually is right for you. A wholesome look at yourself and your aspirations will help you define what is absolutely right for you. Perfect is not ever going to happen, so forget that shit. Well, that is a bold ass statement, right? Well, let it sink in. Close your eyes, draw in a deep breath, and understand perfect is a figment of your imagination. Holy shit, this guy is telling me I will never be perfect. Sound like the subliminal message playing in your head? Well, it should be, and buckle up, cupcake; it is going to be a rough ride. We live in a world that society tells us we are all equally awesome and everything is just peachy and hunky dory. Well, I hate to break the news, Captain, but peaches rot.

I want you to think of everything that was told to you growing up about events and the outcomes. I know from my experience it was beautiful how it turns out: You will go to school, grow up, get a job, buy a house, have a family, and retire to your countryside home in harmony. Sound about right? That self-reflection I spoke of, go ahead and give it a shot. Tell yourself what you're doing, where you are at, the goals that were assigned to you as a child, school, family, $60,000-a-year job, or anything I might have missed. My guess is, most of you reading this are probably just like me, and this is a place where you give out a brief sigh. After all, I pretty much just blew up your depiction of life, your childhood, and crushed the perfect dream for you.

Okay, now that we have taken a moment and probably feel like shit, let me tell you something. We overcome this, and I promise, you will overcome that feeling we all have in our guts of insecurity, self-worth, and expectations. Yes, I did just yank out the bottom blocks on your Lincoln Log set, but before you can rebuild, you have to understand that it can be rebuilt. Sometimes, you just step on those freaking little bastard logs along the way. Ah, now you understand the level of pain it takes to get through the rebuild. Life, in the beginning, just feels like stepping on those in the middle of the night. Yes, it hurts like a bitch, but guess what? It goes away and then it's fine again.

Have you ever gone to the store and looked at someone getting out of a huge truck or a fancy sports car? Every single one of us have been a witness to this, and every single one of us always thinks the same things: *Well, that guy is compensating for something, Midlife crisis is happening,* or *That person right there has more money than brains.* These are all our quiet thoughts sitting there staring, maybe even a touch jealous. Perhaps, we should look at this in a different view. I myself still pass these thoughts seeing this happen today if I am being a hundred percent honest.

After facing so many of the trials of life, I really broke down these images, and I encourage you to do the same. I, much like the common person, do not have the small fortune it takes to own that little sports car or the means to take care of the monster truck previously described. However, take a good look at that person, because perhaps, just perhaps, they are playing chess while we are looking for our checker pieces. I stated earlier that rocky road just is not ice cream. I encourage you to think about this deeply. Could it be possible that this person is compensating or has more money than brains? Why, sure, it could. However, what if this person just went through that rocky point in life? Once you reach that crucial changing point in life, things change. Maybe they have understood this all along. There could have been a life-altering event that already knocked over their proverbial Jenga tower. Perhaps that truck or sports car is this person's new first brick when they hit that moment. The cornerstone of a new future if you will.

The first step really is not admitting it or acknowledgement of it. What it really is, is understanding it. I myself worked and worked to overcome everything life threw at me and at times to the point it was dangerous to my very own life. I did all this to obtain what I thought then was the dream house, family, perfect career…blah, blah, blah. I simply was doing everyday things and stepped on a piece of glass. That right there a piece of fucking glass is my life-changing, wake-up moment.

Glass? You stepped on a piece of glass, and it changed your life? Well, that small piece of glass had something on it that caused a crazy infection, and I lost my left leg. Something as meaningless and trivial as a small cut could be your moment. Believe me, it got me good. What you really need to do is look at whatever your moment is or was and understand it. The rocky road of life has many up and downs. The first step of your rebuild starts with grasping that concept. Now, you may ponder, what does understanding this moment have to do with the rebound? The answer is, *everything*. For me, I was so busy with work and structure of my life I just continued on like I always do. It was a small cut, so I cleaned it, slapped a bandage and Neosporin on it. Sure enough, it scabbed, healed up, and everything seemed kosher. Eventually, after some time, I started to feel off, and I went to the doctor. At the doctor's, all of these things were discovered, and I had to have my leg amputated or I would certainly face death in a matter of hours.

Holy shit! There I was, a young man in my thirties, faced with the worst circumstance you could ever imagine. Sure, I have faced adversity, failed, had success, lost friends/family, and even began to build toward this goal of the American dream. Nothing—and I mean *nothing*—else matters when you hit this moment in your life. One thing I must clue you in on, and I feel it is my obligation to do so, is the mere fact no pep talk will ever make your situation easier.

The world fills you with so much bullshit and false positives that it is hard to actually decipher anything of value. Only once you understand that your situation is unique to you and you alone, can you move forward. You must come to terms that Preacher Bill and his miracle spritzer of water followed by a bop on the head is not the answer. You are the answer and the only answer. Understanding that your moment really is just that a moment. In my moment, there was not even time to formulate a plan of action. I had to act now or there would not be a way to continue forward. All that kept running through my head was, everything I had done and accomplished is over. What the fuck, how did I get here? I worked my ass off to get ahead, to beat the taxation of blue-collar life. Goddamn it, I was close too. In fact, this year was supposed to be the year that I could taste the fruits of my labor. Yet all this had just happened. I, at first, was like anyone would be and had the why-me attitude. Then I began to understand this instance. I had spent so much time chasing a fairytale that I lost my life in the mix. I spent all my time working and abusing my body just to achieve this unobtainable goal. I set my own bar so high that I neglected all of the adventures along the way. The bumps and bruises from that rocky road of life are actually beautiful. They all are meaningful and have a minor impact to a larger result. This giant event is merely the boulder in this rocky roadway of life. Once you get an accurate depiction of what it actually is, give up on the simple thought of hope, you will become motivated for yourself, and then you will understand how to overcome. I began here with the sharpest point because it cuts the deepest. Simple fact is, it fucking hurts, it's a bitch, it is not going to fix itself, and you are in control only after you accept that. The key thing I wanted you to take out of the opening here is it sometimes the world is shitty and there are many obstacles of everyday life. The biggest hurdle is the one that will make you appreciate the little ones that you overlooked along the way. My own ignorance led me to overlook these things, so now I am going to show you, through my stupidity and dark sarcastic life, a basic strategy guide. Life is a mind-fuck full of philosophy, nostalgia, bumps, bruises, letdowns, and learning. Now bite your lip, bend over, and get ready to dig into some real complex shit that really is not real complex but complicates life.

It's Dark...So Mote It Be

Well, as you have figured out, I am not going to sugarcoat things and tell you deep breaths and meditation will cure what ails you. Hell, I am not going to tell you that ales will cure what ails you. The first thing for me was to understand that life is dark, full of mystery, misery, and your happiness only comes from within. Now, do not misunderstand me, the shit is dark, and the rain cloud may follow above your head, but once you accept that, you will learn to love the rain. Life itself is not all sunshine and roses. We see more dark, ill, and uncanny things naturally because it is all around us. Do not believe me go ahead and watch the news for a half-hour. Tell me how many good stories you hear because I know it will not be many. My point here is to accept the dark and use dark humor to better grasp your reality. Learning to find the comedic value in life's crazy times will lighten your mood so much coping will become easier. Humor: it's the first piece that you need to take out of that mental kit.

There is no greater tragedy endured by man than the Holocaust, although that has not halted comedians from cracking jokes about it for decades. Neither have audiences thought twice about laughing at such jokes. Take, for instance, Larry David's classic *Curb Your Enthusiasm* 2004 episode, which was rooted in Solly, a Holocaust survivor. On one of the nights, Solly attends a dinner party with the hopes of meeting a fellow Holocaust survivor. Due to an unplanned mix-up, Colby Donaldson—one of the survivors from the reality show—arrives instead. There is a heated debate between Colby and Solly regarding the more enduring survivor. Solly states Colby could not even fathom the level of suffering during the Holocaust and that he could not compare her suffering to his. Colby responds by complaining that he was unable even to work out given there was not even a gym. People ate this shit up, and the audience loved it. The point here is each was a survivor but in different means, as are we all. Right from being the little swimmer from your father that made the connection. There is a certain comedic value to everything, and that is the true building block right there!

Given that people can find comedy in tragic events as horrible as genocide implies that anything people can find humor in practically anything, given that it is correctly presented. All throughout history, the greatest thinkers have made a note of this rare tendency to shine a light on dark moments. According to Plato, mixing pain and pleasure brings rise to humor. Similarly, Mark Twain also stated once that "humor is tragedy plus time." Psychological researchers have discovered why mankind is able to find humor in tragic situations and how efficient comedy is at helping people cope during stressful times.

Researchers have noted that humor is born out of negative circumstances. This discovery seems to be counterintuitive, but for obvious reasons: how does something so potentially good or bad give rise to something so good? Some researchers have made efforts to illuminate this question in various papers that *Psychological Science* has published. Researchers have explained that the benign violation theory can give answers to the query. This theory's basis is that people's amusement can also be attributed to moral violations. Take for instance, threats posed to their conventional ideologies of how they view the world around them but only if such violations do not pose any threat to their well-being. When a playful tonality is employed in the threat, or a harmless setting is used, a violation that could have potentially evoked fear or depressive moods leads to laughter. Each of us as a person will experience something like this and actually feel this. I myself stepped on a piece of glass that had some bacteria on it that got in my blood and nearly killed me. I lost my left leg and visited with the reaper himself. Yet I pulled through and reverted to humor in a negative situation. Now only a few months have passed and humor has helped me cope, from funny shirts mocking the injury to my new Christmas story leg lamp. Yes, it may be inappropriate, dark, harsh, and many others, but it supports this concept.

According to theory, a factor responsible for the transformation into harmless jokes of such threatening violations seems to be psychological distance. This distance is divided into four categories: Spatial distance (tragic events on Mars are less likely to affect minds on Earth), social distance (if a relative is a Holocaust survivor, that event might more likely be troubling than amusing), temporal distance (challenges faced the previous day might be different from those that happened decades ago), and mental distance (hypothetical situations do not pose a threat like real ones). Regarding the benign-violation theory, the success or failure of a joke depends on its unique blend of psychological distance, moral threat, and emotional safety.

Comedy has a such a fine sweet spot where the correct level of threat is needed. The two ways humor can prove to be a failure is if it is boring and/or offensive. One of the ways that sweet spot can be achieved is through psychological distance. Circumstances characterized by benign violations proved to be funnier compared to those that had malicious violations or benign actions that were old and generic. Researchers have found proof for such occurrences across five experiments. In one of the experiments, student subjects were exposed to pairs of scenarios rated individually in terms of the degree of humor and threat they possessed.

Among these scenarios was one of a young girl aware of his father's job loss and the money issues. The girl decided to respond to this situation by auctioning her virginity on eBay. Close to 80 percent of the test subjects considered that response as "wrong," although 45 percent claimed that it evoked laughter out of them. Concerning the paired scenario, the same girl takes the action of selling her jewelry on eBay. There were no participants who found this action to be a violation, but it was also not considered to have comedic value as well. In simple terms, people more likely than not found a situation funny if it both posed a threat to their conventional worldviews and did not come across as excessively severe.

When researchers attempted to discover the impact that psychological distance had on molding moral violations into benign formations, they found out that humor was dictated by distance in two ways. When the tragedy was immense, a more significant psychological distance was necessary to consider the event harmless enough to pass as comedy. Insignificant setbacks, which begin as mildly benign, do not require a lot of distance to maintain sufficient threat to have humor in them.

McGraw and colleagues (2010) conducted five studies to explore the benign violation theory further. In one of the experiments, the emphasis was placed on psychological distance and its temporal aspect. The researchers first asked test subjects to explain what event they would more likely consider being funny: being run over by a vehicle long ago or being run by a vehicle the previous day. Sure enough, concerning the car accident degree, 99 percent claimed to require a distance of five years to consider this incident humorous. Following this response, the researchers replaced the car accident with someone being stubbed on the toe. Out of five participants, four stated that such a less harmful incident had a high likelihood of being humorous even if it occurred the previous day.

Another experiment emphasized the component of psychological distance. In this experiment, McGraw and colleagues explained to test subjects that a woman had donated $2,000 by accident to a charity group through text message. The test subjects considered this costly mishap funnier when they felt that they were not related in any way to this woman than if the woman was a friend or a close relative. When the mishap only cost $50, however, there was a reversal in the outcomes. This time, the innocuous mishap was funny only if it happened to a close person. Psychological distance acts as a mediator of the level of how wrong something might be and the level of how okay something might also be.

Apart from benign violation theory's cause of humor suggestion, it also explains one of its usual implications, which is the idea that jokes aid all of us in better coping with life's hardships. Being able to laugh during stressful moments enhances the reduction of negative emotions associated with the event and develops positive feelings connected to amusing events. When combined, these two effective swings are responsible for an individual's coping abilities. According to Arnie Cann, a person becomes more efficient in their coping when they can utilize humor to alter their perspective on matters and perceive a possibly threatening event as posing less threat.

The notion that humor can heal can be traced to the Bible—according to the book of Proverbs, for instance, a merry heart is as effective as medicine—although the lab did not investigate its direct impacts on stress until the late 1900s. Reports made in 1981 by Herbert Lefcourt and Rod Martin in the *Journal of Personality and Social Psychology* claimed that humor helps people better cope with stressful episodes in life. Following these claims, there have been several empirical studies proving from time to time that humor helps relieve stress.

Cann got himself into the field following a request to carry out training drills with emergency medical workers who had stressful tasks due to tragic events. He discovered that these employees regularly had to cope with the work's emotional strain by utilizing humor (although they were ever keen not to display their humor in front of the patients), as Cann pointed out. This just goes to show the relativity of psychological distance. Cann stated that in some situations, a joke might be necessary for aiding everyone to cope with the fact that they have experienced a very stressful event. According to these workers, humor was vital to their occupation and their survival.

Cann, in one of his early research, he and his colleagues exposed test subjects to two videos. One of the videos, called "Faces of Death," contained graphic images of compiled fatality scenes; the second one revolved around stand-up comedy. (A neutral video was viewed by a selected control group instead of the stand-up comedy video). Later, an assessment of the participants' moods and emotions was done following the videos' impressions as reported by these participants. The outcomes provided the suggestion that humor's coping implications are astonishingly flexible. After test subjects watched the comedy video before the violent one, the funny video positively raised their moods. Additionally, it shielded them from the negative effects of the violent scenes.

When test subjects viewed the disturbing footage before watching the funny one, there was still a positive rise in their moods, although they were still left with some anxiety. Cann and company made conclusions regarding the preventive or curative traits of humor toward stress—although it works better as a preventive mechanism.

It is important also to note that there is only so much that humor can do to act as a medicine for stress. In his paper titled "Current Directions in Psychological Science," Rod Martin (1996) analyzed the belief connecting physical effects such as illness, reducing blood pressure, tolerance to pain, and longevity to humor and discovered that this connection was flimsy at best. According to Martin, humor and the health benefits it affords the body as a result of laughter did not have conclusive evidence as people tend to believe commonly.

Regardless, empirical studies still show that humor, as a psychological coping mechanism, reduces stress and anxiety in people. According to Western Carolina University's Thomas Ford, laughter is incompatible or inconsistent with fear and anxiety. Ford goes on further to assert that people who can be humorous even during difficult episodes of life are, without a doubt, better off. A recent experiment by Ford and colleagues discovered a new way to measure the effectiveness of humor in its inhibition of anxiety. Ford and colleagues brought test subjects into a room and stressed them out after informing them that they would be sitting for a complex math test. Later, some of the subjects were instructed to read John McPherson's newspaper series, *Close to Home,* and were instructed to read ten comics from it, whereas the remaining participants read ten poems or nothing at all.

The subjects that were exposed to humor scored substantially better than the rest, in addition to feeling less anxious about the test. There is a big difference in the stress associated with a math test compared to the stress connected to a big event like the Holocaust. The fundamental principle about humor's protective attributes is still clear. Extrapolation from the research has shown that human beings handle stress better through humor to reduce emotions associated with anxiety. Mankind will, in time, be able to make light of almost everything.

Does a joke have the ability to meaningfully make a difference in the way people perceive their friends and colleagues? Studies have shown the answer to be a resounding yes! These results do not come as a surprise, though. This is because most people feel that humor is vital. When test participants were asked the qualities that attract them to their colleagues or partners, most stated that among other factors, a sense of humor was at the top of the list. Although when the same people were asked to state the character traits they thought a leader should have, humor was not a primary factor.

People tend to view humor as a secondary trait for being a leader.

Humor is, in fact, a formidable device that is instinctively utilized by some people, although it could be wielded with more purpose. Having a good laugh with friends at social events, or even better, in the work environment, encourages cheerfulness, enhances communication at an interpersonal level, and creates social bonds. According to examinations regarding sets of communication at the workplace and at social events, humor is used in not less than 10 percent of the emails and has a high likelihood of being used by keynote speakers and leaders during face-to-face communications. These figures might be and should be even bigger. Research has proven that humor has the potential to prompt and strengthen group hierarchies, build prime quality relationships and interpersonal trust, and essentially mold people's perceptions of their friends' competence, warmth, confidence, and clearness in communication. Additionally, humor and sarcasm affect crucial attitudes and behaviors that are important regarding leadership effectiveness, including job satisfaction, citizenship behaviors, job performance, organizational commitment, psychological safety in social groups, creativity, and future longings to interact again.

However, jokes that are considered dull or offensive (they come off as ill-timed for the context) can be detrimental to professional standing by making the joker less competent and less intelligent. It can lead to a drop in prestige, and in worse cases, cause people to lose their jobs and friendships. This section provides a guide on ways of using certain humor variations to become a much more successful leader and friend—and how to prevent being branded as a person who other people should be cautious of.

There is an intricate connection between humor and laughter to power and status. Individuals who do not possess a high rank and can carry out themselves properly can climb the status ladder within their organizations and departments. People who make appropriate and witty jokes have a higher likelihood of receiving nominations for leadership positions by their colleagues. Recent experiments have found that the connection between status and humor is so strong that simply motivating people to recollect a humorous exchange with a colleague altered how they perceived their colleague's status.

In addition to aiding people to climb up the authority ladder, humor also makes them effective leaders once promoted. When leaders utilize humor as a device for interpersonal relationships, the workers are more jubilant, promoting better communication and leading to a positive deviation in citizenship behaviors—charitable activities that enhance organizational effectiveness. When a leader utilizes humor, there is a higher likelihood of workers to go above and beyond their responsibilities.

According to researchers Peter McGraw and Caleb Warren (2010), humor usually takes place when something is considered a nonthreatening violation. They carried out experiments in which test subjects were put under situations where someone was depicted doing a benign activity (for instance, a successful jump being completed by a pole-vaulter), an infringement (for instance, an unsuccessful jump by a pole-vaulter, which leads to a serious injury), or both (a failed attempt by a pole-vaulter, who does not necessarily injure themselves). Test subjects who witnessed the third setup were much more expected to laugh than those who watched either the first or second scenario. According to the researchers, things are considered humorous if they induce the feeling of unease but do so in a manner that is agreeable or not excessively threatening.

Given that joking about things that threaten our psychological well-being can be considered risky, it can potentially paint individuals as more competent and confident. Whether or not a joke is perceived as inappropriate or efficacious, test subjects made out the joke tellers to be more confident because they were courageous enough to tell the joke in the first place. Such a display of confidence leads to a higher reputation (given that the audience does not have any prior perceptions implying a deficiency of competence). It was also discovered that individuals who violate norms and expectations in a more socially fitting manner are recognized as more intelligent and competent. This outcome reinforces the notion regarding funny conversationalists: their humor and wit are respected and admired, which increase their stature.

Humor's profane nature sometimes is what renders it dodgy and risky. Jokes that go way overboard the suitability line have just the unparalleled impact—an "eeek" reaction. Instead of perceiving the joke teller as competent and intelligent, the audience has an unfavorable reaction and views the person as an idiot. Regardless of whether an inappropriate joke teller is viewed as confident, reputation can be lost due to the low competence indicated by failed attempts at humor. Furthermore, studies have confirmed that unsuccessful humor can cost leaders their status, rendering them even much shoddier than serious, unfunny leaders who have never made any effort to tell a joke totally. It can prove complicated to find equilibrium between an extreme violation and benign violation, even skilled comedians regularly get criticized for crossing the line—and it requires expertise to get it right.

During conversations with other people, it is necessary to balance several motives concurrently. It could be an objective to swap information with clarity and accuracy, impart a positive imprint on each other, and circumnavigate conflict, among other things. The level at which each motive is perceived as normal and socially appropriate is different from setting to setting. For that reason, context plays a vital role with respect to humor. It is much safer to talk about a funny tale concerning the awful hotel service experienced overseas to friends or colleagues during a dinner party (where enjoyment is the normative motive) than to tell it to a border patrol agent while coming back to the country (where swapping of information is the normative motive). A given gag might work exceptionally with one faction of individuals but flop with another. It could still bomb with the former group if the context is different. Although witticism (with good intentions) fundamentally serves the social glue role, they could hold the opposite result if they are taken out of context and are viewed as thinly masked boastfulness or an insult to a certain group or ideologies.

This type of witticism occurs anytime an outside party does not have the information background required to comprehend the joke. Inside jokes are particularly popular. It is important to understand how insider jokes influence a group's dynamics. In a study to ascertain these influences, participants were asked to take part in a brainstorming assignment via instant messenger. Every participant was made part of a team, with some researchers disguising themselves as fellow participants. In one setting, one researcher delivered a message to the group that was hard to be interpreted by the team (it appeared to look distorted), and a response was sent by the other researcher stating, "I agree!" The other participants felt like these two researchers had exchanged information that they were not in the know about. In another setting, the second researcher gave a response in regard to the distorted message by texting back, "Hahaha, that is ridiculous, I concur!" It was a slight variation, but in both settings, test subjects were on the outside. Was it important whether they did not get the joke? Yes. The test subjects had a higher likelihood of believing that their team members had a superior feeling concerning the inside-joke setting than the inside-intelligence setting. They stated that there was diminished group identification and unity when exchanged confidentiality was a joke.

Most people have undergone this experience personally. Despite the notion that fun is perceived as behavior that enhances strong relationship bonds, it can create fault lines within a gathering, causing a feeling of exclusion or awkwardness within some people. Inside jokes do play an important role, of course. They can indicate camaraderie or closeness, making individuals have a pleasant feeling of being in the loop. This type of wit can be important during nonconsequential or transactional circumstances when it is not a significant matter whether or not an outsider does not comprehend it. But the results from the studies conducted on this type of humor are distinct: when the cohesion of a group is paramount, crack jokes are understandable to everyone.

According to various researchers, sarcasm is not only used by teenagers attempting to annoy their parents and friends, teams can utilize it, and managers as well. In a study by Li Huang and colleagues, test subjects were asked to make or accept sarcastic remarks or make or accept honest ones. Participants in the sarcasm setting had a high likelihood of substantially resolving a creativity assignment designated to them later during the experiment than participants in an honest setting. In another study that followed, test subjects were requested to simply recollect a moment when they either stated or overheard a sarcastic comment or a time they overheard or stated a sincere statement. Once more, creativeness on the successive task was greater in the sarcasm setting.

What causes this? Sarcasm is about talking of one thing but implying the opposite, therefore, its use and interpretation need abstract reasoning of the highest degree (in contrast with a straightforward assertion), heightening originality. The demerit is that higher degrees of perceived conflict can occur, especially when there is minimal trust between the recipient and the conveyor. And given that sarcasm is about stating the reverse of what one implies, there is a misinterpretation risk or worse in the event the receiver is unable to pick up on the intention of the humor and literally perceives the sarcastic statement. The lesson: let your sarcastic side show so that creative juices flow. However, it is advisable to bring it down in the presence of new acquaintances, under unfamiliar settings, or when performing tasks with teams where strong interpersonal bonds are not yet formed. It is safe to use sarcasm with people with whom you have formed a strong trust; otherwise, it is advisable to communicate with respect.

John F. Kennedy was faced with allegations regarding his wealthy father's efforts to buy the election during Kennedy's presidential campaign. Kennedy, during the 1958 Gridiron dinner party, spoke about the alleged accusations by stating, "I just received the following wire from my generous Daddy: Dear Jack, don't buy a single vote more than is necessary. I'll be damned if I'm going to pay for a landslide" (John F. Kennedy).

Humor that is self-deprecatory or overly modest can prove to be a useful approach during the neutralization of negative claims about an individual. People are perceived as friendlier and more competent when they choose to reveal negative allegations regarding themselves using humor than talking about it in a somber mood. When humor is attached to a confession, people perceive the negative info as less important and less true. For instance, various studies have revealed that job candidates who disclosed their math inability in a witty manner (for example, "I can subtract and add, although I draw the line on geometry") were viewed as being more able to do math in comparison to those who revealed the information in a humorless manner (I can subtract and add, but I find geometry to be intricate").

There are boundaries, however, to the advantages of self-deprecating humor. With respect to individuals of lower status, it could fail if the skill or attribute in question is a vital area of competence. For example, an arithmetician can get away with making a self-deprecating joke regarding their handwriting than her skills in arithmetic and statistics. Therefore, when talking about fundamental capabilities, a different form of wit might come in handy. It is only right to be serious when disclosing an inability in a self-deprecating manner regarding a core competency. Additionally, it is safe to steer away from utilizing humor to disclose shortcomings where cheerfulness would be viewed as inappropriate (for instance, when testifying in a court of law) or in the event that the weakness is viewed as extremely severe that making jokes about it would be seen as crass. During the White House Correspondents' Dinner in 2004, then-president George W. Bush displayed footage in which he was examining the Oval Office and talking about the weapons of mass destruction being somewhere around the office, maybe under some object. This subject matter was extremely substantial for jokes, and unsympathetic criticisms ensued because of the video.

During the United States presidential elections of 1984, the incumbent, Ronald Reagan, was asked during a debate whether his age would hinder his proficiency as the president for the second term. At seventy-three years old, he was presently America's oldest president, and people viewed him as being weary in the first debate. The president responded that he was not going to make age be a severe matter to the campaign. He further claimed that he was not willing to take advantage of his opponent's inexperience and youth for political gain. Walter Mondale, Reagan's opponent, along with the audience, burst into laughter. Mondale later stated that it was at that moment that he realized he was not going to win the election.

Not many people prefer being asked complicated questions similar to the one Reagan had to answer. Prior research has shown that there are a variety of ways individuals can provide responses: by maintaining quietness, openly being deceitful, paltering (speaking the truth for misleading), or using a different question as a response. Using humor to evade a query is an additional option, which may prove useful in specific events. This is due to the distracting cognitive nature of humor. Like the way a skilled magician gets their viewers to turn their eyes away from the sleight of hand, an effective joke can shift the audience's attention away from specific info. Effective witticism makes people happy, and there is a higher likelihood for trust to be fostered with people during a pleasant mood. As previously stated, funny individuals are perceived as more skilled and intelligent. One of the reasons for Reagan's successful response was because of the attack on his mental capacity. By using a little wit to respond, Reagan showed the audience that his mental faculties were still in check.

Following General George B. McClellan's failure to strike General Robert Lee, Abraham Lincoln was infuriated during the American Civil War. Lincoln talked about the matter inside a note he sent to McClellan, stating that if McClellan had no intention of using the army, Lincoln would have liked to use it for a bit. He ended the note by saying, "Yours respectfully, A. Lincoln." Adopting humor in the delivery of negative feedback, as Lincoln did, can make reproach more unforgettable.

Conveying negative feedback can prove to be a daunting task. Thus, it may be enticing to fall back on a joke to improve the room's tone. However, expressing negative feedback jokingly can soften its shock factor. Peter McGraw and the company conducted experiments whereby test subjects examined complaints delivered in either a grim mood or humorous manner. Despite humorous complaints being taken lightly than serious ones, they were also perceived as gentler, with individuals not feeling very coerced to take steps toward rectifying the issue.

Given that escorting reproach with humor mollifies the feedback, the purpose of conveying the message is undermined when the matter is not apparent. Suppose an employee makes a joke regarding the deteriorating performance of a subordinate. In that case, the worker might feel like his work has not really been diminishing or that the matter is not a big problem. If it were an issue, in the employee's opinion, the manager would not joke about it.

On the day that followed the 2016 United States presidential election, there were two scenarios: it was a day of jubilation for Trump's supporters, but a sad day for Clinton's supporters. With respect to these two scenarios, the researcher took it as an opportunity to analyze how humor might help people handle the undesired news. Researchers asked individuals on Clinton's side to come up with something meaningful or humorous about Trump's triumph. The people who chose humor in that incident felt more elated at the time—and they even felt better weeks later after the researchers checked upon them.

Humor could prove to hold so much power during attempts to cope with stress, even during the harshest situations. Studies have shown that American war prisoners in Vietnam regularly utilized humor to overcome the harsh circumstances they faced. Test subjects were exposed to photos depicting negative images (like bodily attack or a car accident), followed by a positive or funny provocation. Participants subjected to the witty stimulus claimed to have lesser negative feelings than participants subjected to non-witty ones. This phenomenon is that the cognitive attribute of humor creates a distraction within people, rendering them less able to pay attention to adverse material.

Generally, humor can aid individuals in managing stress in the event of an immediate negative event and in the long run. Test subjects who could generate witty responses about negative stimuli (like reacting to a picture of a man with stitches all over his face by saying, "At least he gets to have an awesome Halloween costume") claimed to have a greater positive effect days later when they were shown the picture once more. So, the next time you come into contact with undesirable news such as stalled sales or a failed presentation, come up with ways of laughing it off, even if the words are in a thought-form. As observed by several comedians, it is impossible to laugh and be afraid all at once. There are many ways in which we, though not comedians, do this in our everyday lives. How many times have you went to grab your keys and knocked them off the damn table or tried to hurry and jammed your toe on the corner of something? One usually screams some variations of profanities and chalks it up to Murphy's Law and moves on. Ah yes, Murphy's Law. The next valued piece of my piss-poor guide for you.

CHAPTER 4

MURPHY'S LAW

So welcome to the party Generation X and above we are about to get into a subject based off a sitcom. You remember those right? A television show that portrayed real life through characters on screen to give us said humor and morals. Those were back in the day, and the anxious millennial youth reading this probably only know *The Fresh Prince*. The focus right now is from one of those sitcoms: *Murphy Brown*. For those of you who do not know, that was a show in the late '80s to '90s. Watching this show in my youth, I really thought this show was full of life advice. I had convinced myself this was why Nana and Mom always said Murphy's Law after something happened. Mind blown, right? You're welcome, my age group. That is not why the popular saying became a thing. Understanding the saying, "Anything that can go wrong will go wrong," or Murphy's Law became a household saying. Knowledge of the historical beginning will help you understand how it incorporates into your life

The History and Background of Murphy's Law (Outtakes by Murphy)

Edward Aloysius Murphy Jr. came into the world in 1918 and was involved in World War II as a pilot. He was not very popular during his deployment in the war. Although after the war, his life took a turn when he trained to become an engineer. He became known for his famous and creative innovations. He went on to take the position of an R&D officer working at Wright-Patterson's Air Force Base at the Wright Air Development Center, assisting in the development of emergency frameworks, inclusive of multiple inventions in the area of human centrifuges. These centrifuges were tasked to test an astronaut's or pilot's tolerance and reaction to experiences of acceleration tests outside the Earth's gravity realm—a test popularly referred to as High-G training.

He was part of a special project in 1949 called the high-speed rocket sled. This project was dubbed MX981, and it was aimed at testing the impacts of super speeds on humans and on equipment that was either excessively dangerous or excessively sensitive to be utilized on a plane. These experiments were necessary to design ejection seats that were used in supersonic jets and in rockets that were launched in space. Existing ejection seats were being used before the Second World War, although they could not endure high speeds that ranged from one thousand to two thousand kilometers per hour. Using such seats for ejection at those high speeds would be the equivalent of jumping without a parachute.

How can the impacts of acceleration be tested on ejection and equipment? According to John Stapp, by using a railroad track mounted with a rocket sled some kilometers long. John Stapp, a courageous physicist and a colonel in the United States Air Force, was in charge of this research project. He had various recorded breakthroughs in his experiments to study the impacts of braking and acceleration on bodies. These experiments were conducted at California's Edwards Air Force base, at initial speeds of hundreds of kilometers per hour, followed by more than one thousand kilometers per hour. Following the sled's stop, the researchers determined ways of enhancing the harnesses after ascertaining the level of injuries on Stapp's body. This was done so that amount of injuries would be significantly reduced next time.

The poor Stapp completed every test run with bruised skin, hemorrhages, and more. People speculated that Stapp chose to be his own guinea pig, given that experimentation with animals yielded inaccurate results, and he did not wish any other person to be injured in these experiments. During the early stages of the tests, Stapp was well-aware that the sled did not give precise figures and that the research resulted in invaluable statistics. It was fun soaring objects and people at speeds of hundreds of kilometers per hour, but a bit pointless if the desired outcomes were not obtained. Stapp and his colleagues did not have sufficient information to develop a seat that could endure supersonic ejection speeds. His need for a professional prompted him to bring in the skills of Edward Murphy. Without a doubt, Stapp made the right choice in selecting Murphy. Murphy was responsible for the development of efficient devices for the United States Air Force. These tools were used in the preparation and examination of ejection and emergency systems. One of his designs involved a system containing sixteen sensors connected to the test pilot's strap-ups and belts to provide information regarding their state. Initially, Murphy's innovations were aimed at centrifugal testing, but following Strapp's approach, he seemed more than willing to adjust it to fit the needs of the rocket sled.

There were multiple alterations done in the last minute of the morning during the initial tests back in December 1949. An ape was used instead of strapping Stapp to the rocket seat to not lose a great scientist in the event of a fatal accident. Stapp, however, decided to spare the monkey eventually and took its position in the hot seat. The rockets were put into the ignition, and the sled went down the rail until it came to a steady stop. Murphy, alongside his team, quickly ran down the track to observe the sensors' readings, but to their dismay, they did not find any recording. With the astounding engineer that Murphy was, he quickly comprehended that an error was made. Every tool was examined, verified, and approved multiple times before the experiment to prevent any cause for malfunction. Murphy was surprised to discover that each of the sixteen sensors was incorrectly plugged into their outlets to the instructions he had provided his technicians. The sensors were fixed upside down.

Following this mistake by his technicians, Murphy angrily referred to one of his technicians, stating that "that person will make a mistake if he has any way of doing it." That statement was soon connected to Murphy. Murphy's Law was later eventually summarized to "if it can happen, it will happen," and labeled for Murphy by his workers as a way to mock him of his arrogance. In the book, *The Making of a Scientist*, author Anne Roe presented Murphy's Law to other people around the globe, in which she stated the physicist's law, which stated that "if anything can go wrong, it will."

Murphy went on with his promising career and focused on effective strategies for emergency systems testing. He was part of several ambitious projects in the US inclusive of the

Apache helicopter, Apollo spacecraft, and the phantom jet. But historians are doubtful of whether or not Murphy's Law should use the physicist's name. Nevil Maskelyne, a British magician in 1908, stated that everybody in the world has the shared experience, that on any given special instance, for instance, when attempting to create a magical effect in public for the very first time, everything might go haywire and will go haywire. Maskelyne did more than just entertain people. He also took part in engineering and was the first person to hack in the world. He hacked into the wireless telegraphy system, which Marconi invented in 1903, disapproving Marconi's private and secure communication claims. Evidently, Marconi did not think that things would go sideways in such a manner.

Discussions were held earlier regarding a version of the Law inside Alfred Holt's 1877 report. In the meeting, the panel concluded that "anything that can go wrong at sea generally does go wrong sooner or later, so it is not to be wondered that owners prefer the safe to the scientific." The long-distance steamship which revolutionized the world's transportation can be attributed to Holt. Claims have been made by Augustus De Morgan—a renowned mathematician—that he invented the Law's principle. He stated in 1866 that the initial test already provides an illustration of the theory's truth, established by conducting several drills; whatever can happen is bound to do so if we do enough practice.

So what lessons can be obtained from Murphy's experiments? For more than 140 years, people with great minds have made attempts to utilize logic in providing explanations for why things go amiss for anybody at any moment. Their quotes sound similar, given that they were all victims of the same problem: even the most brilliant mind in the world is just a human and mostly depends on other humans. And concerning Murphy, following his death in 1990, his son stated that his father did not like how people perceived his Law. If a person missed his flight, they would say to themselves, "Curse you, Murphy's Law!" In the eyes of Edward Murphy, that sounded like disdain. In his opinion, such unfortunate events resulted from a failure to strategize and not a misfortune that just happens even after careful planning.

Fatalism and the Appeal of Murphy's Law

Imagine sitting in bumper-to-bumper, five-lane traffic. The driver is very eager to get to their destination, but they notice that every other lane seems to be flowing except for his. The driver switches lanes, but as soon as they are on a new lane, the new lane's vehicles start to stagnate. As the driver is stuck on this new lane, they notice that all the other lanes on the highway, inclusive of the one they just escaped, are moving but theirs. This is just one instance of the exasperating world of Murphy's Law. According to this law, whatever can go wrong will go wrong. This is not attributed to the law's mysterious power, but it is fueled by the relevance people worldwide give to this law. When life is smooth sailing, little thought is put on it because everyone expects that things should work out by our desires. But in the event things do not go well, people start to bring up reasons.

Take walking, for instance. Many times people get to their destination and think they are superb at walking. But when the individual trips over a step and graze their skin, it is highly likely that they will start to contemplate why that happened to them. Murphy's Law takes advantage of people's tendencies to pay attention to the negatives and overlook the positives. It is like the law makes fun of people for displaying hotheadedness and utilizes the principles of probability to reinforce itself. This law provokes people's imagination.

Murphy's law is a fairly novel concept dating back to the last century's midpoint. In the essay, "On Getting Out of Things," written in 1928 by magician Adam Shirk, the author states that nine out of ten things could go haywire during an act of magic. It was even referred to as Sod's Law prior to this, claiming that any misfortune that could befall a poor sod certainly would. England still refers to Murphy's Law as Sod's

Law. This section will explore the implications of Murphy's Law in the world.

Why do people regard Murphy's Law as a genuine universal concept? For instance, when attempting to fit a two-pronged plug into an electrical socket, there is half a chance that it would perfectly fit, but then again, there is also half a chance that it would not properly fit. Maybe the correct way of explaining people's attraction to Murphy's Law is by examining the basic sense of fatalism. Fatalism is the notion that no one has control over fate's whims. This idea stipulates that man's circumstances cannot be avoided; for instance, the hitherto mentioned bruised knee. It's the concept of there being some type of universal law in operation that takes joy at toying with humans. Fatalism is counterintuitive to another notion—free will. This refers to the idea that everyone has the luxury of free will and that every decision man makes, along with the implications of these decisions, are mankind's own doing.

Maybe the link between a person's life and Murphy's Law is the outcome of fatalism and free will colliding. Murphy's Law, on the one hand, is a revelation of mankind's own unquestionable stupidity. People will make a mistake almost half of the time if given a chance to do so. But that is as a result of man's own choices. On the other hand, man's inability to be in control is revealed through Murphy's Law, similar to the instance of being stuck in traffic on the slowest moving lane.

Murphy's Law does not attempt to prove anything. It also does not explain anything. It only stipulates a maxim: that matters will go haywire. But man is forgetful of various other forces at play during the consideration of Murphy's Law. According to Rudyard Kipling, regardless of the number of times a bread slice falls to the ground, it is always that buttered side that faces downwards. Kipling, the brains behind *The Jungle Book*, observed that most people are relatable with the idea that life is, almost to a laughable degree, hard.

However, with respect to a bread slice smeared with butter on one side, it should be considered that there is a much heavier side than the other. This implies that as it is falling to the floor, the heavier side will twist to face the floor courtesy of gravity, but there won't be another turn back to the top due to similar reasons. So in consideration of Kipling's assertion, he was not wrong—a slice of bread covered in butter will often fall down with the buttered side facing the ground.

Using Mood to Cope with Murphy's Law

Mood and stress are two of the most critical components that are responsible for altering the cognition of Murphy's Law. Negative thoughts can be remolded into positive ones by changing these two components in the pursuit of escaping the consequences of Murphy's Law. Sadly, Captain Edward Murphy Jr., the discoverer of this Law, did not examine these two elements. There is a connection between positive moods and various other cognitive benefits. Positive moods are responsible for the facilitation of several alternative interpretations of particular circumstances (Murray, et al. 1990). Positive moods also enhance flexibility, which is a crucial tool in environmental adaptation, creativity in searching for relevant answers to problems, and utilizing cognitive techniques to aid one in achieving a goal (Murray, et al. 1990).

Positive moods are responsible for people's search for alternative meanings to their undesirable situations. Therefore, when things do not go according to plan, one can adapt and seek another solution. It is not straightforward to switch moods from negative to positive if life is not going following the intended design. However, multiple cognitive techniques can be utilized in the alteration of mood, prevent narrow-minded reasoning, and generally, prevent the consequences of Murphy's Law.

One of the mood alteration strategies involves cognitive coping techniques that call for a person's examination and analysis of their past life to motivate themselves (McFarland and Buehler 2012). Through memory reflection of past traits and achievements, one has the ability to look at their past selves. It is important to note that although there could be an impeccable clarity in memory, not all of them might be accurate (McBride and Cutting 2016). This is due to the non-relievable nature of memories. Memories are reconstructed. A person's current mental interpretations and perceptions can influence how they recall memories and concepts of their past representations. Hence, one's perceptions of being smart and creative rely on how they recall moments when they overcame obstacles like teaching yourself ways of cracking computer codes. However, the only way doing so could work if the person perceives that their personal development and qualities are on the right track. The two factors responsible for altering one's mood, according to McFarland and Buehler (2012), are either derogation or idealization of their past. After examining and idealizing the past-self due to a past ability to solely overcome a complex obstacle, one can alter their mood by recalling the grit and intelligence they used.

Examining past achievements fosters a positive mood by promoting the standpoint that many challenges have been overcome in the past that the person cannot be brought down by anything. The idealized perception of past experiences can alter the mood since it reinforces the person's abilities and capabilities to go through obstacles (McFarland and Buehler 2012). Similarly, a person is able to find motivation through the examination of the past self's derogation by remembering how lazy they were and the need they have now for overcoming challenges. Examining the past self this way can motivate the individual to focus on self-improvement. Through the utilization of such cognitive coping techniques for the alteration of mood, a person can become more creative and adaptive due to the expanded ability to categorize. It can additionally enhance the motivation to overcome complex tasks at the moment. Such cognitive changes have the potential to assist a person in their circumnavigation of Murphy's Law. It is, however, critical to pay attention to the brain's levels of stress since stress breeds pessimism and could possibly render these adaptive strategies useless.

A pessimistic point of view can be attributed to stress. It can influence a person's personality and cognitions. Researchers have discovered connections between pessimism and stress (Shields, Toussaint and Slavich 2016). Shields and colleagues have engaged test subjects in various experiments for several weeks, and they have discovered that stress experiences that were not as severe were associated with changes in personality over time, especially pessimism. One explanation for this occurrence is that stress has the ability to deplete psychological resources and lead individuals to fall down the pessimism hole. Stress has also been linked to impacting various brain facets responsible for representing oneself, other people, and social working memory. Thus, stress has an effect on an individual's life outlook. Repelling pessimism is dependent upon a person's awareness of how stress influences them and looking for means of reducing stress. It is crucial not to allow stress to tamper with cognitions. Failure to do so will lead to the loss of a person's ability to adapt, which aids us to prevent Murphy's Law.

The navigation of stress could prove difficult since it is amassed over time. Deadlines usually add to increased levels of stress. In a single study that examined Murphy's Law, it was discovered that pressure, as a result of time, makes it hard to detect issues (Porter and Smith 2005). This could prove vital in the prevention of things from going haywire. When someone is pressured to finish a task, they might use shortcuts and create bigger problems. Simple issues might then transform into severe problems with little time remaining. An effective way of countering time pressure is to develop comprehensive plans and the active consideration of ways to solve problems if things go awry (Porter and Smith 2005). For instance, it is important to have backups of your work if the computer crashes. Active consideration of the things one can do to prevent undesirable results can reduce life's adversities and assist a person to think of adaptive and creative solutions.

Examples of Contingency Plans for Coping with Murphy's Law

In the event the best-case scenario fails to go through, that should not be an issue because there are various plans in line and on standby. A contingency plan is an alternative way of accomplishing a task. For instance, a man might have made plans of taking his girlfriend to a concert for a date, and after picking her up from her apartment, the rain starts to pour, and the event is canceled. The average male would feel they are in trouble, but a vision-oriented person would not be phased. They would resort to plan B, which could be taking her to the movies. After they get to the movies, they find that the building is at capacity, and waiting in line could take up to three hours.

Most people would consider giving up and going home, but a vision-oriented person would review plan C and take the girl bowling. So what could have been a disastrous date turns out to actually be a memorable night as a result of utilizing contingency plans. Even the backup plan was backed up by an additional plan. Given that the man was thinking of the future, the pivots on his date were smooth sailing. This forward-thinking landed the man a second date as opposed to what would have happened between the two had the night been ruined.

Multiple Lines of Attack

"Lines of attack" is a military term which means a way of accomplishing a task. Having multiple options accords one with the ability to be flexible. People have plans due to their desire to achieve a certain goal, but adjustments could still be implemented on the plan itself, provided that the goal is still attained at the end. For instance, in a castle siege, a defending army might want to topple and take over a castle under defense. There are various routes the army men might take in accomplishing this task. The army can use ladders to scale the wall, use a battering arm to break the gate, dig a tunnel beneath the wall, or starve the defending army. There might be a much-preferred course of action compared to the other ones, but all of them are at the army's disposal. If the first tactic that is utilized proves futile, the army can concentrate its energy toward a different tactic and carry on with the attack.

A common example might be attempting to get to the airport. The individual might arrive there via bus, hiring Uber services, requesting a friend or family member to drive them there, or using their own vehicle and parking it at the airport. There are many options, so just in case the first plan backfires, a different one can be used. To be better prepared for the overcoming of obstacles, it is vital to have more options.

The Negative Domino Effect (to Murphy's Law) and How to Prevent It

Sometimes, negative experiences can be affected by the classic domino effect. This means that one negative situation could possibly alter an individual's day and make it become even worse, which could progress into bigger consequences, and in particular, when the person experiences more personal obstacles. When the degree of stress goes up, the person is not prepared enough to face those challenges and matters continually spiral downward.

Unluckily, the consequences of the domino effect become more costly. The individual then decides to put a stop to these effects and take control of the situation. More often than not, a large amount of money is usually spent on the obstacles so that another party may step in and deal with the consequences on behalf of the affected party. Some instances may include: buying take-away from a restaurant instead of making early plans to prepare a home-made dish; or calling a car mechanic to drive the individual's car to the repair shop that the owner might not even be familiar with; or purchasing a plane ticket at the last minute; or renting a vehicle at the last minute.

No person is immune to the consequences of the domino effect. It is difficult when it occurs because it makes the subject feel like they have lost control over matters due to everything collapsing all at once. Time, plans, and money evaporate, and the person feels stressed. However, hope should not be lost because there is a way to approach the domino effect if it does take place. The solutions can be categorized into two parts—things that can be done in the present moment and those to be planned for later to prevent future domino effect events.

Negative Domino Effect as It Happens at the Moment

In the event that you are in a situation where a myriad of negative events is taking place and accumulating, there are specific actions that can be taken to reduce the negative implications and save money at the same time. Four strategies will be discussed in the subsequent paragraphs.

First, it is important to ask for assistance from your social network. If a person finds themselves in a spiral of undesired events, turning to a network of friends might prove useful. For instance, it might help to ask a friend to babysit for a couple of hours. Maybe another friend could chip in to look after the pets. They can also seek recommendations from another person or request them to stop by a store and pick something up for them. Important friends can be relied upon and come through when their friend is between a rock and a hard place.

They are willing to lend their friend a car or watch after their children and their pets.

The worst possible scenario in investing less than a minute to ask for assistance is receiving the answer no, which only brings the person back to their starting point. However, if the answer is yes, then one problem has been lifted off the person's chest, which prepares them to take care of the remaining obstacles in a mini crisis. Letting go of less critical commitments in the event of challenging setbacks should not be an issue. It should not be a big deal to miss your son's first football trials in school just one time. It is okay to be late to a dinner party by fifteen minutes. It is okay to miss out on a community meeting, etc.

Examining and analyzing the commitments that are being faced is crucial when trying to select the few that are of less importance so that it can be easy to take a step back from them. It will not be the end of the world if these slightly less significant things are not done within the stipulated time. What will be discovered after less important things are taken off the to-do-list is that it becomes much easier to tackle the remaining issues all of a sudden. Consume foods that are nourishing to the body when possible; when buying food from the supermarket, picking the healthiest ones as much as possible will go a long way in preventing the domino effect. One of the most critical elements associated with a negative domino effect circumstance is stress. The mind and the body start to feel really stressed when incidents start collapsing onto one another. Stress on the mind will undoubtedly lead to poor decision-making, possible ill health, and poor emotional response.

It goes without saying that during a stressful incident, it is not possible to just wish the stress away, although the body can be better adjusted to overcome the stress by nourishing it with the right foods. During a crisis, feeding on the right material will go a long way toward the achievement of success because there is clarity within the mind and the body. Sometimes finding "clean food" could prove to be inconvenient. When one is forced to quickly get food, they can drop by the local market's produce area for healthier foods instead of driving by a fast-food drive-through. Instead of fizzy drinks, pick water.

In addition, sleep is important to handle the domino effect. It is advisable to make an effort to get quality sleep every day. Eating healthy and getting sufficient sleep go toward improving mental and physical health and preventing unwanted ailments. When the mind and body feel clear, success can be easily attained. It can be extremely tempting to work during sleep time when one is under stress—staying up for hours during the night to perform various tasks to prevent the feeling of being left behind. The disadvantage with doing so is that the level of productivity may severely dwindle during the coming days, and any perceived progress will be lost.

Negative Domino Effect Afterwards— and Prior to the Next One

The hitherto listed strategies to deal with a negative domino effect at the moment it happens are useful, but the best way to deal with a pile of crisis due to this effect lies in the preparations made in advance so that problems do not come swarming in. It is a given that a crisis will hit at least once. Making preparations for them when things are peaceful will be beneficial in preventing them in the future. The paragraphs that follow will illustrate how one can go about making preparations.

A preferable way of creating an emergency fund, for instance, is through the provision of instructions to the bank to make small amounts of money transfer every time a substantial deposit is made. For example, every time a deposit of $450 is made on the checking account, $45 can be placed inside the savings account. Most banks can carry out such transactions. By doing so, that money will not be spotted in the checking account. There is an efficient and quiet transfer of this money into the savings account, and the individual will not be stressed about thinking of that money until the emergence of a disaster—or a compilation of crises.

Another example could be the advance preparation of quick meals. When a family is consisted with five members or more, buying fast-foods on the run could prove to be very costly in the long run, and it is preferable to avoid doing so. However, there could be instances when grabbing a meal to-go becomes important, especially when undesirable events stack up. Spending money during such times becomes extremely tempting when there are quick meals already prepared. Having multiple meals in the freezer is one way of ensuring food security in times of crisis. Such meals only require reheating and serving. The microwave is another appliance that can come in handy for reheating bags of frozen soups and foods. When one feels lazy, especially on weekends, such foods can be prepared and stored in the freezer to be consumed during normal life on the weekdays.

It is important to use a social network of reliable people who can repair and fix things. These people will prove to be vital during emergency incidents. Examples of such reliable people include, but are not limited to, a reliable local cooling and heating enterprise, a reliable local mechanic, a reliable plumber, and a reliable electrician. These people are not to be looked for during the outbreak of an emergency but should instead be sought when times are calmer. After an emergency experience, these repair people should be sought with the aid of recommendations from friends. What people do these friends use during emergencies? Are they reliable? What price do they charge for their services, and are their prices affordable?

On the other hand, when friends are in need of help, do not hesitate to also extend a helping hand. Helping a friend will also prompt them to remember how you stepped in for them during a difficult time, and they will also not waste time in returning the favor. It is critical to know which friends will help babysit the children, which ones will help when moving out, etc. It is not about expecting assistance in return, but the goal should be to foster strong friendship bonds with as many people as possible. This way, when one is in a sticky situation, they have multiple options of where to seek help. It makes a significant difference during emergencies to reach out to many friends and be able to find a decent number who will be able to respond. Therefore, when life seems difficult for a friend and looks good for the other person, the equation can be reversed.

It is necessary to rethink commitments and put aside the least significant ones. A contributing factor that leads to the worsening of an incident into a crisis is that most people—more so families with kids—place excessive commitments on their shoulders. Then, in case of matters go awry, their house of cards comes tumbling down. If one finds themselves in a state of affairs where even a minute thing can cause the whole system to collapse, it means that that is an unsustainable situation in the long run. This may lead to consistent skipping of responsibilities and continuous failure to meet deadlines with other duties. Generally, it gives off the image that the person is not reliable and evokes the feeling of being overstrained and overburdened.

It is far better to have fewer commitments that are easily attainable for excellence, characterized with increased flexibility if things do not go according to plan. When one is tasked with a few commitments, an obstacle in one sector of life will not begin to disrupt the remaining commitments subsequently. It could be viewed as domino spacing further apart before they are eventually knocked over. Spacing them further apart means that it will not affect the rest when one "domino" falls. Examining the commitments in life will enable the identification of those that do not add much value. That does not imply that these obligations are unimportant or bad, but it is just a way to remind one that they do not have to put all of their heart into these obligations. It is advisable to scale back on those tasks that cannot be given the effort they deserve when committing to them. Doing so could be hard, but the person will be in a much better place in the long run, more so when life gets tougher.

No one in the world is immune to life's challenges, and all of us will experience challenges at some point. An incident triggered by Murphy's Law that was unplanned for can happen and later on complications from that incident might lead to other unexpected obstacles, and before one is aware, their levels of stress might be compounded, and spending money on the issue might cross one's mind just for the sake of feeling like they are in control. The first step is to take a step back and breathe. Utilizing some of the strategies mentioned earlier—like seeking help from a social network, dropping less critical commitments, and staying healthy—might prove useful among many other strategies. When things start to improve, additional strategies that are intended to prepare for future misfortunes can then be applied to prevent the domino effect of Murphy's Law.

Whether it is dropping a buttered slice of bread on the floor or not remembering to bring an extra pencil to the exam room, the disorder can be spotted in every aspect of life. Given this finding, a person must know ways of navigating through the implications of Murphy's Law. Dark humor and light humor are good tools for managing the stresses of life. Life might seem iniquitous at times and that some people have been on the right side of life when, in fact, the deck of cards has been merely shuffled by Murphy. In the event of such thoughts, it is crucial to understand how to go about dissecting the cognitive hurdles that perpetuate and add to negative cognitions. Comprehending pessimism's effects on one's cognitions is crucial in overcoming undesirable situations, particularly cognitive biases like Murphy's Law.

Practicing humor is a tricky dance, and studies on it are still at an infant stage. Researchers have obtained statistic-driven accounts of ways people utilize certain types of humor to counter stressful situations and be relatable to friends and colleagues. Either way, any rule of thumb in the use of wit should include a caveat: context is important. There could be profound disparities in conversational dynamics from group to group, culture to culture, and person to person. Such dynamics are complicated in their navigation and cause difficulties in ascertaining whether the conveyed humor attempt is successful. Various individuals will laugh courteously even when the joke is in poor taste, which generates a feedback loop that is not reliable. Not every effort at humor is going to be a triumph. Appreciation of humor and finding glee in life's irrationalities will go a long way in countering the effects of Murphy's Law. Well, isn't that some shit, there it is! The real Murphy's Law really seems to be present in life, and there is not one person that can refute that.

CHAPTER 5

CONGRATS, AGATHA CHRISTIE! YOU GOT THE POINT!

All right, so now you get the big picture. Life struggles will always be a problem. You do not overcome them; you cope and survive. We learned how shitty life is for everyone; we discussed my takes; we discussed how the common person visits this; life is dark so mote it be; and anything that can go wrong, it will go wrong. Seems kind of fucked, right? Well, this is the process; once you accept it and learn it is what it is, the better your progression of life. You identify the issue, investigate how to get by said issue, develop your plan presuming anything that can go wrong will, put together the pieces, and formulate a plan to use this knowledge. Okay, so you should be thinking that sounds so goddamn generic.

Well, fuck me and my logic, right? It is logical; that is why it sounds so generic to everyone. However, stop and really think about it. When is the last time you really logically looked at your reality? Dark humor in a sense got us all through some pretty shitty times. *Everyone* experiences things that make them say everything that can go wrong will go wrong (Murphy's Law). We have made peace with the fact accepting these things are a part of our lives necessary for moving on. Moving on in life is a tough cookie to wrap your mind around. Many people really struggle with accepting the first few phases of this plan. Once you swallow the horse pill of life and realize you need to understand the last two chapters, you are ready to move on. It is toxic for you to be in a relationship with something that is abusive to you…well, in this case, life is that relationship.

> Toxic relationships aren't just relationships with someone who is bad for you, toxic relationships are the horrible relationship you have with yourself in which you think you deserve this. (Kristen Corley)

To get past these toxic relationship of life means you have coped with the fact it is going to happen one way or the fucking other. Laugh in the face of life because you know you do not overcome it, you adapt and get over it. *Okay, you messed up son of bitch, I get it; life going to get you before you get it.* Sound a lot like your thoughts right now? Perfect, you understand the word play in the title. We are all a little mentally disabled, and now we learn to become accepting, productive adults. Have you ever read *Everything is Fucked: A Book About Hope* by Mark Manson? If not, I highly recommend it because this is the type of reading that will kick you in the hypothetical nuts to help you grow. In this book, Mason states, "When you google 'how to be an adult,' most of the results focus on preparing for job interviews, managing your finances, cleaning up after yourself and not being a total asshole. These things are all great, and indeed are things that adults are expected to do. But I would argue that, by themselves, they do not make you an adult. They simply prevent you from being a child." He is right on the money, and in fact, I would add to the argument, until you accept the dark humor of life and Murphy's Law, you cannot be ready to be that adult. Is it not that old saying from our parents, "That's what separates a man from a boy or separates an adult from a child" lesson a familiar speech that comes to mind? Wisdom is the lesson here, and we learn from life to formulate our organization of life. One would ask, "All right. wise ass. How do we proceed from here, then?"

Organization can be defined as "to make arrangements or preparations for (an event or activity)." Organization—that is the key to putting together the pieces. You do not need that Sunday morning sermon on television. Magical water, any amount of super meditation techniques nor any other bullshit remedy you see online. You have learned to use the aforementioned tools, now organize your life with the newfound view or outtake of life. We do this naturally every single day without even knowing it. I will give you an everyday example of this: I would go into work every morning right about the same time and run to grab a cup of joe. Well, one morning in my daily commute, I ran into some heavy traffic that was caused by a train crossing town. Well, I missed out on the window to get my coffee, and most of you know how well a day goes when you do not get your coffee. So, I reevaluated my situation based on this shitty day and decided it was a necessity to leave half an hour earlier to avoid all this. Guess what Sherlock, I got my coffee and went about my days hereafter unscathed.

Sounds like a really simple and pretty ordinary corrective action there. Well, it should. These are common everyday switches to our organization of life that come directly from our adverse situations. Now, I am no fucking rocket scientist, but it sure sounds like we just got organized on that one particular problem using real life shit we just went through. We identified that issue, looked at the alternatives, laughed because it was shitty, organized our schedule to accommodate and put that plan into action. Color me freaking shocked; we did that without even thinking about it really. Organization of your thoughts allowed you to come up with a corrective action to make that just another shitty Monday story. This is where your mind will automatically go if you allow it. Anytime these awful issues that you face—whether it is a trivial missed coffee, or in my case, a missing leg—surface, give your mind a moment, and it will do this for you. It will calculate and answer your questions and self-doubts. Okay, on to the lesson portion to help you understand my babble. The rhetoric I am about to share might just bore you, but if you really dive in, it really may just help straighten some shit out for you. After all, that is what we are after here.

Being organized is a significant aspect of life that makes life easy by saving time as well as maintain order. Being organized is essential in all fields of our life including school, organizations, companies, hospitals, social settings, government structures as well as our daily lives such as paying bills and remembering significant events. Organization comes as a second nature to almost all people that ensures success in every single activity that we purpose to carry out. Organization significantly influences our lives from how well we perform at our work spaces to how efficiently we are able to carry out our activities of daily living including cleaning and doing shopping. Boerma and van den Brink-Muinen (2016), suggests that life without the skill of being organized can be unbearable with too much stress to bear. Things as simple as throwing trash away makes life easy and healthier.

Individuals, some of whom experience various challenges in life, find being organized a heavy task, making them vulnerable to procrastination that makes their lives pile up with things that were meant to be done in the past leading to stressful situations (Andrews and Withey 2017). Psychologists suggest that being organized in life plays a significant role in stress reduction. Essentially, being organized is used as one of the traits crucial in determining mental well-being of patients especially those suspected to be undergoing psychiatric disorders in mental health. According to Andrews and Withey (2017), mental health specialists suggest that individual's disorganization, piles of things to do as well as unfinished projects, are a major factor contributing to stress and depression. This happens because, as one works hard to clear away the piles of work and projects that seem to never end, the brain gets tired and the body become fatigued. Saxbe and Repetti (2010) argue that experiences and perceptions that people have about their daily environment informs their well-being. Physical features of living such as work spaces, that include features like noise, overcrowding clutter and artificial lights have been proved to influence individuals' moods and health ranging from young children to adults.

Research reveals that well-organized natural environments such as parks and outdoor spaces play a significant role in alleviating stress because they help restore the human mind bringing peace and relaxation (Andrews and Withey 2017). Organized homes act as a place that families use to unwind from their workday stress. Although this happens in most homes, when household work is not well managed an organized home can turn to a source of stress for some people. Both qualitative and quantitative research prove that the transition that happens from work to home might be less restorative for working females than their male counterparts (Andrews and Withey 2017). A cluttered or a disorganized workplace or home influences an individual's physical and psychological health (Andrews and Withey 2017). Lack of proper management and organization at home poses a health hazard, such as fire breakouts, molds, and dust, that risks the health of those living in these homes. Moreover, research reveal that disorganized people are more likely to choose unhealthy foods compared to organized people. Their choices of unhealthy living influence their lifestyles and causes health related complication most of which finally lead to death.

According to Andrews and Withey (2017), several factors contribute to disorganized homes some that are inevitable, while others are viewed as mere decisions by those affected. One of these factors is attributed to individuals who have never been organized before. Saxbe and Repetti (2010) suggests that not knowing how good organization feels makes it difficult for certain individuals to ever want to feel it in their lives.

People who are often very busy, especially those who have highly demanding jobs, might have little time for organizing their lives the way they would feel comfortable. Most of these people always feel incomplete and might experience difficulties concentrating at their workplaces while others might experience stress. Besides demanding careers, other obligations such as family life and community participation, if not well-managed, could lead to disorganized homes.

Andrews and Withey (2017) argue that what people consider as quality of life is determined by how well events, activities, individual interactions, and other aspects of life are able to smoothly flow in a person's life. The promotion of individual's quality of life and their well-being is a central goal in all modern societies inclusive of the many units within them that cannot be achieved without societies and cultures being well organized (Andrews and Withey 2017). Organized societies, despite differences of opinions both within societies and between them, dictate how well-being of individuals in these spaces should be maximized. The universal agreement that the goal itself is worthy to be pursed is a strong indication of cultural and societal organization. Citizen welfare is achieved not only through organized national level governments but also countries, states, churches, service organizations, villages, educational institutions, and many more who purpose to devote their time and efforts seeking to promoting organized systems to achieve citizen welfare. Developing organized communities help people gain a sense of belonging and dignity as well as restore their sense of significance and relevance. Communities that are well organized in terms of activities, governance and leadership, structures and knowledge achieve the goal of living quality lives. Organizing groups in different settings enhance knowledge on building alliances across lines of ethnicity, age, class, race, and groups while recognizing the ultimate strength these alliances can bring to communities (Andrews and Withey 2017). Organizing communities develops a sense of priority to nurture influential leaders from among the members. One significant role of organized communities to specific individuals is that the overall environment where we live influences our approach to situations in life as well as impacts our well-being (Saxbe and Repetti 2010). Well-organized communities will find space for training and learning through action as well as nurturing all rounded persons respected and trusted spokespersons accountable, as well as competent, to participate in the public life of their communities.

Organization in institutions such as schools influence how events run in school and what the learning institution is able to achieve as well as how well the learners perform. More often than not, the school environment contributes a huge percentage of how learners perform. The influence dribbles down to influencing the students' attitude towards learning and their personal life. The most significant skill to possess as a learner is the ability to be extremely organized especially in university and college (Sife, Lwoga and Sanga 2007). Being an organized learner is a critical aspect to help students achieve the best and be productive in class activities. To achieve this, it is a major step for learners to keep an organized calendar of events that they are expected to undertake throughout a particular period of learning. Keeping the record of all the lessons, assignments, class activities as well as other events helps the student reduce stress and manage their time wisely. Good study skills are significant to be successful in learning, but a student who is disorganized will achieve very little despite their excellent learning skills. Being disorganized as a student leads to situations such as forgotten assignments that end up hurting the final grade or cause the student to fail. Organizing events as a learner is also a critical skill that helps students identify areas that they need to give more attention in order to improve. Additionally, students who organize their work are efficient in delivering quality personal assignment because they have enough time to work on homework and assignments without any pressure.

According to Sife, Lwoga, and Sanga (2007), continuous improvement of institutional programs in institutions of higher learning does not guarantee student success entirely. The most significant factors contributing to successful student performance are determined by an individual student. However, an education institution by its mission, vision, structure, and the composition of the employees as well as their competences are likely to alter the performance of the learners to a very high degree. Learning organization and its influences in learning institutions could be viewed from different developmental levels such as regional, global, organization, teams, and individual. Organized learning institutions provide conducive learning environment and use the most effective learning methods to achieve the best. Learning institutions that effectively influence learner's outcome ensure continuous renewal and performance capacity as well as foster servant leadership. These changes are made in all the developmental levels to ensure that the system works to meet the particular needs of the learner. Servant leadership in institutions of learning ensure that students are engaged in leadership that enhances their sense of belonging and offers them an opportunity to voice their concerns (Sife, Lwoga and Sanga 2007). Effective and organized institutions also ensure internal systems are working harmoniously and effectively to delivery best services to the learners. In such institutions, communication throughout the institution is efficient offering students a chance to organize themselves.

Without having a clear guideline of the things that learners are expected to do, it becomes challenging for them to effectively organize themselves to achieve. Collaboration and teamwork are critical aspect of any organization and one that is determined by how organized an institution is. Good leadership, effective communication that ensures efficient flow of information throughout the institution foster collaboration within workspaces.

Awino, Ogutu, and Musyoka (2018) suggest that being organized is an effective tool in reducing stress because it helps an individual avoid the last-minute rush, helping people carry out their activities in a peaceful way. Ensuring organization in multiple areas of our lives helps manage stress levels while improving our quality of daily living. Getting organized to reduce stress cuts across several aspects of life including organizing the house, having an organized schedule of events, organizing our working space, having a plan of what we expect to achieve in life, being ready to put on the extra time to plan projects in an effective way in order to save time and much more. Awino, Ogutu, and Musyoka (2018) argue that living in disorganized environments either at home or in our workplaces drains us energy, finances as well as our time.

Organizing time is another factor that significantly help reduce stress in our daily activities. Well shiver me timbers, right? Most people who rush to accomplish tasks at the last minute are likely to have spent their time doing nothing or engaging in less significant activities. Organizing time to have a clear understanding of what should be done and when it should be done not only saves us time but helps us carry out these tasks in a comfortable and effective way. In order to get the schedule organized, it is significant to remember some few crucial things. It is noteworthy that schedules contain manageable tasks that individuals are able to accomplish without stressing out. Manageable work schedules that are key for both individuals and companies to help manage time. Having work schedules is vital in the current world as recent trends make it increasingly difficult for employees to adequately manage and balance responsibilities of their jobs and families (Awino, Ogutu and Musyoka 2018). Most employees work long hours, and even worse, some must carry work home after the normal working hours. This results to more pressure on individuals and less time spent with families and friends, increasing the levels of stress among people. The cost of living being high in every part of the world has caused several people to either work for longer hours or take up more than one job that threatens the welfare of most people. Research reveal that if human resource management continue ignoring the effects of these trends, demotivation and unproductive workforce stress levels among people is bound to increase. The concern calls for various companies and workforce managements to better organize safe working conditions for employees (Awino, Ogutu and Musyoka 2018).

Being proactive towards achieving an organized life is an effective approach to dealing with stress that can be empowering. It is significant to ensure that one eliminates patterns of common stressors to avoid stress response that causes anxiety and fear. A good example is when a parent seeks to understand patterns of behavior in a child and addresses them rather than dealing with every situation like it is happening for the first time. When repetitive patterns are addressed, behavior is corrected. Being proactive about stress management calls for organized thoughts to understand reasons behind things and addressing the causes rather than the results. Following the current world trends, especially those experienced in working spaces, personal motivation to organize an individual's life is a crucial tool in managing stress and keeping sane. Although corporate approaches to managing stress are available that allow employees personal leave and flexible working time, what individuals do with this extra time also matters (Andrews and Withey 2017). More often than not, employees take time off from their workspaces and engage in activities that are more demanding than their jobs. At the end of the leave, some feel more tired and stressed than before. Ensuring that people are making best use of these opportunities offered by their employers means they must be well organized both in the activities they intend to carry out and their thoughts. Sabbatical leaves are designed for stress relief and personal education. Another substantial element of well-utilized sabbatical leaves other than relieve stress is that they add to individuals' flexibility and raises employee competence and esteem factors that help people be well organized.

In the corporate world, organizational performance heavily rests on the activities of the company and how organized a company can be. Corporate performance is influenced by the flow of information in an organization, collaboration among employees and executive managers, as well as organized workforce. Failure to organize duties and responsibilities results to poor human resource management, poor quality of work, less productivity and loss of resources. Awino, Ogutu, and Musyoka (2018) suggests that when organization are able to organize workflow in an effective way, then productivity is guaranteed. Therefore, it is significant that companies frequently scan their operating business environments and design relevant strategies that ensure well-organized departments and work flow to achieve success.

Just like other fields and aspects of life, being organized meaningfully influences the medical field. Health care service delivery being as challenging field, it influences caregivers in different ways. Service delivery involves commitment both physically and emotionally (Saima and Zohair 2016). Medical practice is one of the fields that employees have no day off or vacations. This means that employees are usually emotionally drained. Possessing excellent working skills as a medical practitioner offers them opportunity to reduce stress, remain emotionally stable, and deliver quality service. One of these skills that help improve medical service delivery is being organized. The benefits of good organization skills are significant and help practitioners be efficient in their caregiving tasks. Being organized in the medical field includes possessing a variety of skills including physical organization, mental organization, and time management as well as organized communication channels. Physical organization in the medical field has to do with ensuring that documentation is done on time and in the right way to save time and for easier access of information (Boerma and van den Brink-Muinen 2016). To achieve these, medical facilities have a well-organized department responsible for filling documents such as forms, bills, medical reports, invoices, and much more. For easy access, most of these documents are labeled and separated in terms of their categories. It is significant for medical practitioners and other employees in medical field to ensure they shred unwanted documents at least once in a week to avoid accumulation of unwanted documents.

This also helps alleviate paper clutter and provide space for organized and effective working.

The stress associated with medical care delivery causes several symptoms that include short-term memory loss, anxiety, forgetfulness, insomnia, and in some cases, depression. Mental organization refers to the ability of medical practitioners to keep their minds focused and present always. This is a difficult task owing to the responsibilities of their career. For them to achieve mental organization, it is crucial to keep an activity schedule to keep them on track. Other than this, understanding personal boundaries, strengths, and weaknesses helps them be organized. Although medical caregivers need to know their weaknesses, it is only necessary to focus on the strengths and keep boundaries where necessary (Saima and Zohair 2016). Keeping their minds focused on the weaknesses leads to emotional drain and hence, poor performance. Keeping their limits alive is also significant to ensure they are organized. In spite of having a huge load of responsibilities in their hands, efficiency comes when employees are able to acknowledge their limits and avoid taking more than they can handle. Another noteworthy point to keeping organized is ensuring that they focus on one task at a time rather than balancing multiple tasks at a time. Writing goals for each day and prioritizing them by determining order of significance helps doctors remain focused.

Consequently, time management plays a primary role in achieving an organized and successful caregiving day. One of the aspects that determine good organizational skills is the ability to manage time. The current world is filled with people who are always busy without time to relax and interact with others. With good time management, I believe people will find time and space to interact with one another and relax. Being organized helps people keep valuable information easily accessible and goals in focus (Saima and Zohair 2016). Lack of proper organization of documents and other valuable information means that people will spend more time trying to get valuable information from various sources. Learning the principle of delegation helps people create more time to carry on their tasks without much stress. Learning the art to be organized guarantees success in the medical field just like other fields (Boerma and van den Brink-Muinen 2016). Using this as an example, human beings in different spheres of life and career can utilize the skill of organization to achieve more, delivery quality, and use less energy in all activities.

Benefits of keeping organized in life cut across our daily lives and our workspaces as well as in different organizations and fields. Significantly, being organized are skills in life that every person should possess because they make us healthier, more productive, and more emotionally fit. Being organized is vital in increasing productivity in every aspect of life including private life, in the corporate world, and in public participation. Institutions such as schools and colleges, churches, organizations, hospitals and companies are able to manage their work force with ease where they are organized. Keeping organized saves time and increases efficiency in workplaces. It also helps in reducing stress as well as ensuring that people are not emotionally drained. When we keep things in places where they can be easily accessed, organize our day-to-day activities, remain focused on what we need to do for the day, and maintain physical organization, then stress is reduced. Other than this, organization helps us meet deadlines on time without any pressure. Individuals who work in areas that involves collection of huge data, those who receive numerous information within a short period of time, know the need to keep organized. Enormous data that is not sorted can be stressful, time-consuming and emotionally draining (Saima and Zohair 2016). Therefore, keeping computer files organized, ensuring that offices are in order, maintaining emotional organization helps people live an easy life and enjoy their daily activities.

Okay, so maybe that is all a touch extreme, but you can see the value a little bit of organization can bring you now. Everything in life will make a little more sense with this knowledge. Do not mistake that comment for life makes sense because I hate to burst your bubble, but it never will make any sense, but at least you can cope with that internally. Building that step-by-step, organized plan will lead you past anything. I lost a leg, and my entire life was flipped upside down. After using the first few things I explained to you, I began to organize a new plan. The hardest part often in understanding it all. My big life organization was to simply get a fucking hobby.

Getting a hobby can really be a self-organization tool. Hear me out, I promise to make sense of that statement. Now, I understand that life is fucking stressful, jammed pack with chaos, kids, family, strife, and on and on. A hobby will help you unintentionally organize your chaos known as life. Find something you truly love to do—knitting, hunting, reading, fishing, jogging, drawing—whatever it may be, find it. Got it? Okay, now let's look at your life and designate some time to it. For me, all I did was work. When I finished working, I found more work to struggle through daily activity to occupy time. That made me more fucking miserable than you could ever imagine. I needed that hobby, and I found it in the Freemasons. The Freemasons provided me with the necessary nutrition to feed my appetite for normalcy. It gave me a purpose, something to do, and a way to challenge myself mentally. To look back and laugh now is easy because I got it organized into a beneficial plan. I reorganized my entire life around my hobby. The hobby has brought me new friends, things to do, a more open mind, and above all else, a way to cope with all the bullshit that runs downhill. Organizing your life around something that makes you happy really helps with positive vibes. Everything—even though I am disabled, both slightly mentally and physically—has become better through these basic principles. I promise if I can make it out of all this, so can you! You simply laugh, cope, organize, then bend over, bite your lip, and grab your ankles. Perhaps understanding and creatively organizing this chaos of life will help.

CHAPTER 6

GET A F——KING HOBBY

Well, now if that does not really explain the next portion, I guess the large build up was just wasted. There is only so much more one could build up to this for the simple fact a hobby that fits you clearly affects your quality of life. If you do not believe, verify with my fiancée for my path to learning this. For those of you that dig information and proof for my obnoxious rant here you go! Once you have discovered the use of this in your life, I promise you it will change for the better. So why should I get a just get a hobby? I assure you this is not a new gimmick from Ronco.

With the increasing number of mental health disorders and suicide rates, mental health is gaining popularity as an important determinant of overall health. Choosing and engaging in the right hobby serves as a significant relief of psychological stress, which improves the individual's mental health. Further, the right hobby brings improvement in an individual's mood by stimulating the release of endogenous endorphins that results in better moods among these individuals. Veterans who have psychological disorders such as post-traumatic stress disorder (PTSD) engage in hobbies to improve their symptoms, although not just veterans experience PTSD. You could say, you know, you have an accident and lose a leg, for example. Further, choosing the right hobby has been implemented in children with neurocognitive disorders such as autistic children. In these children, the therapist chooses a hobby to implement in play therapy to improve these children's symptoms. Students with a good hobby usually perform better academically because it serves as a way of mental relaxation. Not only does the hobby bring about improvement in the quality of life due to the improvement of mental health, but it also results in an overall physical and social well-being of the individual. Through the promotion of social and physical well-being in addition to mental health, the hobby thus guarantees the health of the individual and, in turn, returns to a better quality of life. The socialization (huge piece to the puzzle reacclimating happens) that results from practicing the hobby is important in creating new opportunities and allowing one to interact with individuals of different ethnic, religious, and social groups. Through socialization, one can learn important things. Further, some hobbies, such as jogging, serve an important purpose of promoting physical well-being by preventing some lifestyle diseases such as obesity and coronary heart diseases. This portion really will shed some light on how choosing the right hobby can improve the quality of life by assisting to relieve many health conditions, relieving some symptoms of already existing mental disorders, and increasing overall performance. This is the meat and potatoes of your daily living; sure, we all work and work to…there it is…the cat has your tongue. The answer is to provide, to belong to have a purpose. Our quality of life is made up of all these things. A hobby suited for you directly impacts this.

Do you know you can achieve health and prevent many diseases by simply choosing a good hobby? According to the World Health Organization report, health is not merely the absence of disease but rather a state of social, physical, and mental well-being, which can be achieved by, to some extent, choosing the right hobby. Since time immemorial, many people have neglected mental health as an important element of an individual's ongoing health. With the rising number of suicides resulting from psychological distress, mental health is gaining popularity as a vital health element in the contemporary world. There has been a notable increase in mental health disorders, further making mental health gain more popularity. The answer to good mental health seems to largely lie in simply choosing the right individual's right hobby. Another crucial reason for choosing the right hobby is that it has been shown to bring remedy even to children with neurocognitive disorders, making their mental health status improve considerably. For instance, choosing the right hobby for an autistic child and implementing a play therapy hobby has significantly improved these individuals' symptoms. Their communication skills and overall behavior improve (Karube, et al. 2016). Further, the right hobby has been shown to bring about a significant relief in psychological distress among individuals under a depressive state, with the result being that these individuals record an improvement in symptoms and, in turn, a reduction in the number of suicide cases.

Additionally, another impact of the right hobby is that there is an improvement in the individual's mood, and most of these individuals are generally happy when engaging in these activities. Tomioka, Kurumatani, and Hosoi (2017) state that there is a significant scientific basis that underlies the improvement of moods when one engages in the right hobby. The authors further explain that engaging in the right hobby results in improved symptoms because there is a release of endogenous endorphins that improve the individual's mood. In addition to mood improvement, individuals who engage in the right hobby have performed better academically because engaging in the hobby serves to offer relief to these individuals. The result is that they can concentrate better on their studies;

they record better results academically. Additionally, the veterans, who have received experience inequity in mental health access for quite a long time due to lack of special psychological care, thus leading miserable lives, have been advised during psychology sessions to choose the right hobby to help them relieve the psychological distress. Yigitcanlar, et al. (2020) state that the veterans usually suffer from some serious mental health disorders such as post-traumatic stress disorder that usually result from the traumatizing experiences they witness in their career line. The authors further state that the engagement in the right hobbies serves to distract them from thinking about those experiences most of their time, and the result of that has been shown that they record improvement in symptoms.

Choosing and engaging in the right hobby contributes to improving quality of life by improving mental health and contributing to the physical and social well-being important elements of health (Morgan, Hourani and Tueller 2017). Engaging in the right hobby serves to create an interactive platform whereby the individuals can socialize during the hobby. Through socialization, an individual can interact with different ethnic, religious, and social backgrounds, thus gaining diversity. Further, through social interactions during the hobbies, the individual gets a chance to get exposed to other opportunities such as job opportunities. Most importantly, engaging in a hobby serves an important purpose of attaining a proper physical status. Physical status has been recorded as the most common cause of obesity among contemporary world populations. Thus, it has engaged in activities such as jogging, bike riding, and nature walks. Weightlifting serves as an important way if preventing obesity. In addition to preventing obesity, engagement in the right physical activity serves as a way of preventing other lifestyle diseases such as hypertension, coronary artery diseases, among others (Peráčková and Peráček 2019). Thus, considering that the right hobby improves mental, social, and physical health, which are important elements of health, it is explicitly clear that choosing the right exercise is key to improving the quality of life.

Mental health has, for long, been neglected as an important factor that influences the health of an individual. Still, it is gaining popularity and importance, with mental fitness being regarded as more important in the contemporary world. Proper selection and engagement in the right hobby are some of the most effective ways of maintaining mental fitness that influence an individual's health. Without proper mental health, an individual's health is not considered complete (Yigitcanlar, et al. 2020). There has been the invention of so many hobbies ranging from jogging, reading novels, nature walks, car rides, weightlifting, listening to music, among many others. Each hobby comes with incalculable benefits, leading to many people being unable to choose between hobbies (Tomioka, Kurumatani and Hosoi 2017). However, the selection of the hobby should simply be based on the one that brings the most mental peace because mental fitness is gaining popularity day by day. In the past few decades, there has been a considerable rise in the number of deaths resulting from suicide that has prompted the government to formulate ways to deal with the rising number of deaths. One of the measures has been implementing some gaming time in the school curriculum to help the child relieve the psychological stress that results from the pressures that come with schoolwork. The gain of the momentum of the campaigns aiming to advise people to engage more in exercises has resulted in many people meeting the World Health Organization criterion for determining the individual's health that usually emphasizes the social, physical, and mental well-being of an individual.

According to a report by the Centers for Disease Prevention and Control (2019), the number of children suffering from neurocognitive disorders is rising. Engaging these individuals in some activities is an effective way of improving the symptoms in these individuals. Yigitcanlar, et al. (2020) hypothesize that the increase in children suffering from disorders such as autism spectrum of disorders, attention deficit hyperactivity disorder, and cerebral palsy is increasing in number at an alarmingly high rate that is necessitating the formulation of measures to help these children thrive through their education colliculus smoothly. The authors further explain that some effective ways engage these children in hobbies that they show interest in. Morgan, Hourani, and Tueller (2017) ascertain that through this method, the children can develop a strong bond with their caregiver, with the result being that they can open up to them more comfortably. Through that, the educational professional can identify their problems and offer proper intervention for them. Additionally, play therapy is effective in bringing about symptom improvement in these autistic children. The therapist should identify hobbies that the child shows interest in because the kind of play that one engages the child in is crucial in determining whether the therapy's intended goal will be achieved. Engaging these children in the right goals results in the child recording some improvement in symptoms such as communicating better and improved socialization skills. The overall effect of implementing the hobby in these individuals is that they can navigate better through the school program recording better academic achievements.

Depression has for quite some time remained a major killer in the contemporary world, and psychologists seem to have found a remedy in play. Peráčková and Peráček (2019) assert that the psychologists are now emphasizing engaging the depressed individuals in play as a way of disrupting the cycle of thoughts that usually lead to depression in these individuals. The main principle surrounding depression seems to lie in the thought processing process. Tomioka, Kurumatani, and Hosoi (2017) put it that by engaging an individual in some favorite hobbies such as bike riding, playing football, or even nature walk, the cycle of thought process is distracted, resulting in improved symptoms in these individuals. The limbic system is essential in the processing of emotions and has been isolated by scientists as an important part of the brain that plays a vital role in the causation of depression. Further, by engaging depressed individuals in various hobbies, they feel more appreciated in society and serves as a way of relieving the psychological stress (Peráčková and Peráček 2019). Failure to engage these individuals in favorite hobbies results in their depression, running into intolerable psychological distress that ultimately culminates into suicidal ideations. Morgan, Hourani, and Tueller (2017) explain an increase in the number of suicide deaths among depressed individuals. The psychologists emphasize the importance of engaging depressed individuals in their favorite hobbies to help them attain a proper mental health status vital to a healthy being. Thus, choosing the right hobby can serve as therapy to help depressed individuals relieve stress.

The mood is another important element that is significantly influenced by engagement in the right hobby. Taking part in the right hobby makes an individual attain good moods that makes one enjoy life more. Participating in hobbies such as jogging results in the release of endogenous endorphins that act on the individual to result in a happy mood. Thus, instead of using a pharmacologic intervention or drug abuse to attain better moods, one can simply engage in the right hobby because engaging in the right hobby ensures that the individual achieves the desired happiness and there are no underlying side effects. In contrast, using pharmacologic therapy to improve one's moods comes at a price because the individual has to experience the adverse effects of the medicine that he takes. Additionally, using drugs, such as heroin, is associated with a lot of risk of massive mental damage. Thus, engaging in the favorite hobby to improve one's moods is the safest way an individual should practice because other ways come with many disadvantages. Tomioka, Kurumatani, and Hosoi (2017) highlight that moods are controlled by the limbic part of the brain that is majorly associated with controlling one's emotions. Thus, the improvement of emotions stems from the brain, releasing several endogenous components. Thus, exercise brings about general improvements in moods that, in turn, results in a better quality of life.

In the contemporary world, school curriculums have been largely modified to create children's time to go out and play. The playtime creation results in an overall improvement in the individual's performance (Yigitcanlar, et al. 2020). The playtime allows the child to engage in the hobby of one's choice. Through engagement in the hobby, the child can relieve the psychological stress that results from reading pressures that the child goes through. Further, the child can gain new skills from their classmates, such as playing football skills. School should serve an important function of promoting the children's talents and ensuring students' academic excellence. Also, the set-aside time is important for those who like telling stories as their hobby. By telling tales, especially historical tales, and listening to others, the hobby serves as an important tool for cultural transmission because the children get well-integrated into the culture, which is one of the school curriculum's main goals (Morgan, Hourani and Tueller 2017). Additionally, the children who have a well-balanced schedule usually record better school performances than those whose schedules emphasize full-time classroom reading. Thus, one advantage of engaging in the right hobby is that children with better hobby engagement usually record better academic excellence.

For a long time, the veteran has been subjected to inequity in mental health access due to a lack of specialist mental health programs to alleviate their symptoms. Still, currently, the psychologists advise them on hobby involvement to achieve symptom relief. Most veterans usually suffer from severe mental health disorders such as post-traumatic stress disorders that usually result from the traumatic past experiences that these individuals experience and head injuries that they acquire in their line of duty. Post-traumatic stress disorder and other mental disorders lead a miserable life due to nightmares, among other experiences. Tomioka, Kurumatani, and Hosoi (2017) state that the result of that is that those individuals are likely to suffer depression. Studies have also shown that these individuals have more marital conflicts and their spouses find it a great deal living with these individuals (Peráčková and Peráček 2019). As a remedy to this, the psychologists advise their spouses on engaging these individuals in some favorite hobbies. By engaging them in those hobbies, there is a general improvement in symptoms because these individuals (Morgan, Hourani and Tueller 2017). The improvement in symptoms usually results from these exercises disrupting the flow of thoughts among these individuals. They are likely even to get less hostile when engaged in the right activity. However, these individuals' engagement in hobbies such as nature walks is usually given as an add-on therapy to the pharmacologic therapy because hobby alone cannot achieve the desire alleviation in symptoms

(Yigitcanlar, et al. 2020). However, it is crucial to adequately couple pharmacologic intervention with counseling advice such as hobby involvement to achieve the targeted results.

Knowledge is power, and from engaging in hobbies such as reading novels, one can acquire knowledge. Some hobbies, such as reading, are important in neurocognitive development because the brain's continuous utilization has resulted in more cognitive development than those who barely study. Further, some other educative hobbies that one can engage in include discussing recent technological innovations (Morgan, Hourani and Tueller 2017). The result is that some individuals develop an interest in researching further about certain things. The effect is that most individuals choose to engage in research concerning those things. The result is that there are more technological innovations. Further, such hobbies help achieve a knowledgeable generation, and the effect is that there is a larger economic growth recorded by the generation (Tomioka, Kurumatani and Hosoi 2017). The dependency level of an educated population lowers because the population can acquire some jobs and work for themselves and thus a lower economic burden among these populations. Additionally, most technological innovations result from individuals who developed an interest in technology and invented something new. In addition to resulting in an increased quality of life, engagement of the right hobby can result in innovations. The individuals will have a passion for whatever they are interested in.

In addition to engaging in the right hobbies helping one attain proper mental fitness, hobbies have greatly helped achieve physical well-being in most individuals. The World Health Organization emphasizes the physical well-being of the individual in addition to the mental well-being. When properly coupled with nutrition with high calories, physical inactivity has been the major reason for the increased prevalence of obesity among populations leading to poor life quality. The poor quality of life usually stems from the complications that arise from obesity, such as obstructive sleep apnea, hypertension, coronary heart diseases, and stroke. Engagement in the right exercise can remedy all these because physical activity significantly reduces individuals' risk of developing obesity. Some of the hobbies that can help in reducing the prevalence of these lifestyle diseases include some strenuous exercises such as weight lifting and morning running (Peráčková and Peráček 2019). Additionally, those who do not like engaging in strenuous activities can engage in jogging and nature walk activities because they also serve an important function of burning calories. After all, it is essential to avoid the accumulation of excess calories in the form of fat.

Additionally, hobbies that entail exercises are important because they help prevent other lifestyle diseases such as hypertension, coronary artery diseases, and other diseases (Morgan, Hourani and Tueller 2017). The type of hobbies that an individual engages in usually depends on the availability and affordability and the individual's demographic location. The hobbies of individuals living in rural areas vary considerably from those living in urban areas. Thus, in addition to its being a form of enjoyment, it is an important way of promoting the individual's physical well-being. Some exercises such as weightlifting contribute to the burning of excess calories, resulting in significant prevention of lifestyle diseases. The result of this is that there is an improvement in the quality of life of the individuals.

Further, engagement in the right hobby impacts health because it contributes to the individual's social well-being. When one engages in most types of hobbies such as jogging, running, dancing, and swimming, one gets to socialize with other people. Most of the individuals that one gets to socialize with are from different ethnic, social, cultural, and religious backgrounds (Morgan, Hourani and Tueller 2017). The interaction thus helps build diversity that helps the individual compatible with living with people of different groups (Tomioka, Kurumatani and Hosoi 2017). Additionally, through socialization, one can learn and appreciate new cultures and other important things from their people. The result of that is that the people are equipped with working with people from different backgrounds, and thus, they can thrive better in workplaces with complete diversity. Additionally, through the socialization during the practice of the hobby, one gets to know new individuals and is exposed to more activities. The result of that is that individuals can get some new employment opportunities from the people they interact with (Yigitcanlar, et al. 2020). Further, socialization is important for the children because it helps them integrate into the cultural practices that enhance their ability to thrive better in different cultural backgrounds. Further, the children get to appreciate that there are different cultural backgrounds, and the effect is that there is a reduction in violence resulting from cultural disparities (Peráčková and Peráček 2019). The result is that the quality of life is improved because, through the interaction, one can get some friends in his social circle to share ideas with (Karube, et al. 2016). Thus, engaging in a hobby creates a platform for one to interact with other people from diverse ethnic, cultural, religious, and social backgrounds that promotes diversity in the individual, enabling them to get acquainted with some skills to enable them to thrive in organizations with a diverse composition of employees.

To conduct my research on how getting a hobby can improve the quality of life by influencing an individual's social, physical, and mental well-being, I first prepared a draft of my research paper. I then jotted down some of the claims I have heard from various sources, such as a hobby that can greatly impact children with neurocognitive disorders; veterans usually require special mental attention. Choosing the right hobby has proved to be quite impactful. To further clear doubt on the claims I had heard and gain more information regarding my study topic, I opened some search engines with the most trustable information such as PubMed, Centers of Disease Control and Prevention, and Google Scholar. From these sites, I was able to obtain quite a several articles on my topic. Since the search results were so many, I decided to narrow down my result by focusing on the articles peer-reviewed within the last five years. The number was still quite high, and to further narrow down my search results, I concentrated on the English version articles only. From the final search results, I selected the articles that seemed to be most promising and those that had all the relevant information to my study. I first skimmed through all of them to ensure that they covered all my topics of interest. After that, I carefully read through them and then commenced my study. Throughout my study, I kept on revisiting parts of the article that had the information I needed, and I collected quite a several important data from the articles.

Some of the articles' important findings were that mental health was not regarded as important in historical times because health, by then, only entailed a mere absence of disease. However, from various studies presented in the articles, I appreciate that mental health gained popularity as a vital determinant of health due to the increased number of mental disorders. Choosing the right hobby was essential in bringing about symptom improvement among these individuals. Further, I found out that children with neurocognitive disorders benefited greatly from choosing the right hobby because it led to a notable improvement in their symptoms, such as communication skills and developing some interest for others and the overall surrounding environment. Also, I found out that the veterans were leading a worryingly miserable life due to the poor mental conditions they acquired in their line of duty. I noticed that most psychologists advocated for these individuals to choose the right hobby because it significantly improved symptoms. The results also indicated that spouses of veterans engaged in the right hobbies had a notable improvement in symptoms.

Additionally, from the research study, I found out that children from schools that allowed playtime for the children generally recorded better performance than those from schools whose curriculum did not embrace play's importance. Engaging in the right hobby further resulted in a significant improvement in mood through a process with a complex underlying scientific basis, and individuals who regularly engaged in their hobby of choice were generally happy most of the time. Another finding was that some hobbies such as reading or venturing into technology were reported in the great acquaintance of knowledge and led to many technological innovations. Further, I found out that the right choice of hobby did not only bring about symptom improvement due to promoting mental well-being but rather plays a great part in promoting social and physical well-being. I found out that engaging in jogging, weight lifting, and playing football resulted in a decreased prevalence of lifestyle diseases such as hypertension, obesity, and coronary artery diseases. By choosing the right hobby, I also found out that one can build social well-being that stems from interacting with people from different ethnic, social, and religious groups.

There is a gain in popularity of mental wellness as an important factor because it has been neglected for so long that it has reached a point where the cases of suicide are increasing at an alarmingly high rate. Concerning this, the rehabilitation centers have looked at the matter with an inner eye to formulate ways to relieve psychological distress and improve symptoms among these individuals. Engagement in the favorite hobby has been identified as one of the cheapest remedies, which one can implement to improve symptoms among individuals suffering from depression. Further, the improvement in symptoms that results from play therapy in children suffering from autistic spectrum disorders can be attributed to the play creating a connection between the caregiver and the child. The advantage of the strong bond created between the two is that they can open up more freely to the caregiver. The caregiver can understand the child's problems and conduct a goal-driven therapy to improve symptoms in those individuals. There is a notable improvement in symptoms recorded in school children who engage in their favorite hobbies. Academic excellence can be attributed to the play's ability to offer mental relaxation in these individuals (Karube, et al. 2016). With proper mental relaxation, the children can retain more in their memory when they study and an increased concentration span for these individuals. Allowing the children to play freely is important because it helps them record some growth in their talents. The increased innovations that have been recorded have resulted from supporting individuals interested in technological research because by supporting these individuals, they can achieve greater heights and gain more knowledge on their topics of interest.

The veterans need special attention and care because they suffer mental health disorders that usually necessitate special care. The understanding that the veterans usually had more marital conflicts and the repost from the spouses that they experienced challenges living with them was because the soldiers experience some traumatizing experiences and head injuries that lead to mental disorders. These individuals usually experience some challenges when they retire, and they, in turn, result in more marital conflicts among these individuals. By engaging these individuals in their favorite hobbies, there is a notable alleviation in the individual's negative symptoms, such as being in a constant state of depression and reducing family conflicts. Thus, in these individuals, psychological support such as helping the individuals identify the hobby that fits them most is essential in enduring that they do not suffer intolerable psychological distress. Another finding was that conducting mass campaigns to advise people on the importance of choosing a favorite hobby led to a notable decrease in suicide rates. The significance of this is that pharmacologic intervention alone is not enough therapy for depressed patients. It should be adequately coupled with a favorite hobby to achieve the best results. With such proper coupling, the individuals record improvement in symptoms, and the likelihood of individuals experiencing suicidal ideations is significantly reduced (Morgan, Hourani and Tueller 2017). Additionally, the prevention of lifestyle diseases such as obesity that comes with engagement in jogging, running, and playing football can be attributed to the exercise's ability to reduce excess calories and prevent them from accumulating excess fats.

Further, the exercise can promote the individual's social well-being because it offers a platform for people to socialize when performing their favorite exercises. The result is that they interact with people from different backgrounds. The effect of that is they can appreciate the cultural differences better that enhances the social skills of the individual. The scientific basis behind the improvement in moods recorded in these individuals is that it leads to the release of endorphins that, in turn, results in a generally happy mood in the individual. Thus, from the research findings and the discussion, it is clear that engaging in the right hobby contributes to mental well-being and positively impacts social and physical well-being.

Conclusively, children with neurocognitive disorders should be assisted and engaged more in hobbies to improve their symptoms because play therapy is effective in these individuals. Further, the veterans should be assisted in choosing the right hobby to alleviate the symptoms they experience due to their traumatic experiences from their line of duty. Through this, the veterans will be receiving equity in mental health access, improving the quality of life. Further, educational professionals should embrace the importance of allocating enough playtime in the school curriculum because it should promote academic excellence and ensure that they integrate into the culture. The children with adequate playtime in their schedule usually record better academic excellence because play serves an important role in offering mental relaxation. Additionally, the psychologists should embrace nonpharmacological intervention when treating depressed patients because the adequate coupling of medication and hobby engagement leads to a notable improvement in symptoms. The individuals that usually get bad moods should be advised to try engaging in their favorite hobbies as a way of getting symptoms improvement because through exercise, the brain releases endorphins that result in individuals getting happy. Further, the research indicates that educational professionals should be keen on developing the school curriculum because it considerably influences their performance. With a proper school curriculum, the children are likely to perform better because they will not suffer from mental fatigue.

Additionally, it is explicitly clear that choosing the right hobby can serve as a gateway for innovations. Some hobbies, such as understanding more about technology, usually make it possible for them to make further innovations in the field. Thus, children with such interests should be fully supported to endure achieving the best in that field. Engagement in neurotic activities such as a frequent reading of novels leads to decreased chances of developing disorders such as dementia at old age. So some hobbies can serve to protect one from some severe mental disorders. Further, it is clear that conducting mass campaigns to advise individuals to choose the right hobbies can serve an important function of decreasing the prevalence of some lifestyle diseases such as hypertension, coronary artery disease, and obesity. The result would be a considerable decrease in the mortality rate resulting from these individuals and an overall improvement in the population's health. Additionally, social well-being is equally important to mental and physical well-being for an individual to be considered healthy. The state social wellness can be achieved by ensuring through socialization that occurs when engaging in a certain hobby. The result is an overall improvement in the quality of life of the individual.

This study's future implication is that professionals dealing with children with special needs such as autistic children should be trained more on how they can engage these children in hobbies to improve these children's symptom improvement. Further, equity in mental health access for veterans should be guaranteed. Thus, psychologists should emphasize how engaging these individuals in the right hobbies can alleviate symptoms and, in turn, improve the quality of life among these individuals. The research also indicates that more emphasis should be placed on the school programs' educational professionals to ensure they understand the importance of play and its impact on children. Further, the future school programs should be inspected to ensure that each curriculum has set aside adequate playtime for the children because it results in better academic excellence. Additionally, encouraging depressed individuals to engage in the right hobbies is likely to improve symptoms among these individuals and, in turn, a decrement in suicidal rates. Thus, the psychologists should advise depressed individuals to engage more in their favorite activities. With the positive effect of preventing several lifestyle diseases, healthcare providers should advise the genetically predisposed individuals to engage more in exercises to reduce the risk of developing diseases.

The future should also support children whose hobby is like understanding more technological issues. That is likely to contribute to more innovations in the future in the technological field and all fields. Additionally, the schools should conduct some activities such as football events at both local and national levels to create a socialization platform. It prepares the child to work in organizations with more diverse groups of individuals. Further, the research creates a gate for more future research that aims to answer questions such as: what exact mechanisms in the brain do engage in hobbies result in improvement in symptoms in patients with mental disorders? Are the effects of engaging in hobbies similar to all individuals? If there is any difference in how individuals respond to different hobbies, such as physical health improvement, what really contributes to the differences? Is there any genetic control on how individuals' bodies respond to engagement in various activities such as exercises, and if so, what genetic genes are implicated in the influence? Thus, this research serves as a gateway for many researchers to research further because some concepts still need further research to understand how a hobby can serve as a therapy form in many psychological disorders. In addition to the research influencing the future performance of many professionals such as psychologists and caregivers to children with special needs, it offers insight into areas that need to be researched further on anyone who wants to venture into the field of research.

Well, there it is all the reason you could ever want to go find something to do. Now, I know my real life interaction with finding this said hobby took me forever. I did not just wake up one day and go, "Well, shit. Let us learn to play trumpet today." Not that there is anything wrong with that; if that is your desire, have at it. The point of all this is you need the structure and organization to iron out life, you need the hobby to iron out your mind; therefore, use the one to benefit the other. If you use your hobby to release, it will, in turn, make your organization easier because you have something you *want* to plan for. It is literally icing on your cake that it just so happens that it is good for you too. Every single step I have taken you on to this point all lead down one twisted path to molding your life. Even though life can be twisted and just fucking shot it is possible to develop positively. This tough love guide of sorts will lead you to developing a way to living the best life, as this younger generation so eloquently says.

CHAPTER 7

LIVING YOUR BEST LIFE

Now, I am not going to sit here and bullshit you. By no way, shape, or means is anything really ever going to be your absolute best life. Hell, I am disabled, battered, and bruised so what about that is the best life? Truth is there is always going to be someone out there who you will be envious over (I call them the two-leggers). On the same note, you must understand that you are that someone to another. So this millennial catch phrase that you see tagged on every dumbass Instagram photo and Snapchat filter really is just that a relative saying to an event. However, just maybe there is a point to this catchy saying. Perhaps living your best life is a string of these moments, and putting together these moments is what will make life better. That is the key right there: tying together the strings. Some maybe shitty, some maybe crazy, and some maybe wonderful. Every single second teaches us a lesson, one that will develop our lives and help to aim that moral compass. I really believe that a nice deep dive two feet first into this will help pull every damn thing we have discussed pull together. Aristotle perhaps one of the most famous Greek philosophers once said, "Happiness depends on ourselves." Through all the guidelines and shit I have told you, this is area you must understand to enrich your daily living. We all recognize this from the new hashtags on social media, but the principles are from the ancient philosophers and still relevant today

Everybody aims to be happy and to live a good life. What makes a good life is a complex question that most philosophers have grappled with for many years and various people around the world have their own interpretations too. Therefore, the metrics of a happy life varies among communities, ethnic groups, cultures (like today's pop culture), generations, and individuals. Some people define a good life in monetary terms as having so much money while other see a lot of power as the real source of happiness. While money and power may just be one of the requirements for s good life in the contemporary world, there are so many powerful and rich people whose lives are full of regrets. Philosophically, certain universal facts form the basis for the determinants of a good life. Some people have hypothesized that health, family relationships, and fulfillment. Ideally, human beings need both physical and mental health in order to live a good life, but happiness goes far beyond that.

From Plato, various philosophers have attempted to provide their interpretation of the meaning of happiness and the concept of a good life. However, Aristotle argues that good virtues guide a successful and happy life in addition to physical and mental health. In an attempt to uncover the various determinants of happiness, Aristotle answers different philosophical questions related to a happy or good life. In *The Nicomachean Ethics*, Aristotle explains that happiness the best definition of a good life and should be pursued in the right manner (Smith 2019). We will really illustrate the concept of happiness and illustrate the philosophical explanation behind living a good life and developing a moral compass. According to Aristotle, living well entails consideration of both the end and the means.

The Role of Physical and Health in Living a Good Life

The development of modern medicine has proven that psychological health affects physical health through physical processes like the endocrine and the immune systems. For example, dealing with grief may manifest in the heart rate, which risks a heart attack. Various literature on psychoneuroimmunology has revealed that psychological stress is manifested in the adverse effects on physical health and aging and the positive effects such as happiness, motivation, and a sense of purpose. Therefore, happiness is the meaning and purpose of life. For one to be considered living, they must be happy. In this regard, the connection between happiness (emotional health) and physical health of great importance. Positive psychology elaborates on the relationship between happiness and physical health. Numerous experiments in this field of psychology have shown that happier people have better immune responses and lesser chronic illnesses.

Furthermore, science has proven that the heart is the body's engine, which must determine the level of physical health and activity. Traits of positive well-being are associated with emotional health and tend to determine one's predisposition to heart diseases. Also, optimistic people with minimal stress have high antibody responses. In other words, your psychological health drives the desire for your physical activity and a drive to foster social connections, both of which lead to better health and positive emotions. Mental factors determine a lot about physical function and physical health, from healthy diets to drug abuse. Therefore, mental, and physical health are prerequisites of a good life. Just like ancient philosophers, living morally and virtuously is the key to happiness. According to modern philosophers, happiness involves valuing everything, including one's self and others. Which really makes things stressful and diminishes really what we have known for ages from the great philosophers.

Ancient Philosophy on the Concept of a Good Life

The concept of "a good life" is not new, and many great minds have struggled to define it and inspire people on how to live fulfilled and morally upright lives. Whether it is possible to live peacefully and happily in a world full of uncertainties of war, hate, and economic crises is a question everyone grapples with at some point in their lives. However, the ancient Greek philosophers outlined the golden rules of living a good life, which formed the foundation of today's moral teachings. Even though most of these philosophers disagreed on specific concepts, they both had the same view on what makes a good life. For example, Plato explored the concept of mind and soul and viewed the two separately. Plato, therefore, comprehensively studied the art of the soul and its impact on a person's life. On the other hand, Aristotle felt that mind and soul are intertwined, and one could not exist without the other. However, the two philosophers agreed that the soul connects the mind to the body, a concept that has proven very useful in theorizing a good life.

According to Socrates, a good life is synonymous with just life. As an associate of Socrates, Plato related physical and mental health with virtues and more significantly, temperance. This school of thought viewed a good life as a person that possesses virtues and displays a character in relation to others. Therefore, Socrates held that the virtue of temperance is key to the health of a soul. In this regard, health and happiness depend on the state of the soul. Conscientiously, justice is the one virtue perceived by most philosophers as obligatory for a good life. To avoid suffering from injustices and injuries from others, the best instrument to champion in life is the virtue of justice. Aristotle confirms that the best part of living a good life is living justly. However, Aristotle believes that there are many factors beyond an individual's control that influence the quality of life.

Aristotle on the Meaning of Life

Do people look back on their lives in their deathbeds and wonder if they would change their ways if they find themselves in the same situation? Well, even before death, most people tend to live with a lot of regrets. Aristotle outlines various metrics that can be used to gauge whether we are living our lives well and giving the lives a purpose. In the *Nicomachean Ethics*, Aristotle examines the supreme purpose of a man.

Aristotle approaches the concept of the meaning of life by looking at the goal that is an end-in-itself. *Nicomachean Ethics* concludes that the supreme good is happiness (Klausen, et al. 2019). Aristotle also clarifies the fact that both good and bad intentions are crucial in determining our happiness.

Aristotle believed that living well can be achieved by considering the means and the end. In the *Nicomachean Ethics*, the end of a human is to live a fulfilling life and flourish. (We need to understand that is different per person.) Therefore, all human actions are aimed towards these goals at the end. If someone lives well, then they will not have regrets. However, the question that we cannot ignore is that different people have different living ideas well. Aristotelian ethics comes with a different view that all human desires are the same. However, there are two types of desires: natural desires (intrinsic), which are the same among everyone; and acquired desires, which differ among individuals. Natural desires correspond to natural goods, which refers to things that are good to us, irrespective of our perception. Therefore, according to Aristotle, living a good life entails possessing all those things that are good to us.

Furthermore, Aristotle categorizes the goods into bodily goods and goods of the soul. The bodily goods include health, vitality, pleasure, and vigor, while goods of the soul include knowledge, skill, self-esteem, and honor. Bridging the gap between good life and goods of the soul requires moral character development. According to the *Nicomachean Ethics*, good habits are necessary to live a good life, which is why Aristotle emphasized these virtues. Also, Aristotle suggests that there are various indicators of a flourishing (Klausen, et al. 2019). The first sign is determined to make the best out of their situations and live the best life possible. Such people commit their resources, financial or personal, to help in achieving the most virtuous life.

Another indication of a flourishing life is the choices and actions of an individual. As the saying goes, "Without ethically made principles to guide our lives, there cannot be any difference between human beings and animals." Therefore, living a good life goes beyond physical health and material possession, according to Aristotle, but extends deep into the nature of our interaction with others and how we impact their lives. The ability to make moral choices is thus a particular virtue that every human being must possess. Also, consistency is another aspect of living a good life. People should be true to their course and embrace good deeds, not because of the external rewards that come with them, but because they believe in doing the right thing. Doing the right thing is hard in today's society; just look outside or watch the news.

Happiness According to Aristotle

Happiness is the main concern of every person, and we all have our definition of a happy life. Given the complexity in the definition and determinants of happiness sometimes most people do not achieve this goal. Aristotle is often referred to as the happiness guru because of his unique and practical approach to the concept of happiness. According to Aristotle, satisfaction is an activity and not a state as believed by many people, and an unplanned life is less likely to be a happy one. The *Nicomachean Ethics* approve of alcohol, food, and sex in moderation. Aristotelians believe that leisure is more important than work (Delhey and Steckermeier 2016). He argued that all human actions are geared towards obtaining something, and the ultimate goal of every human is happiness. Human beings are inherently selfish and would never do something that would harm them. However, such activities are meant to achieve a higher objective, which is happiness. Such actions, which are a means to an end in itself, is the highest good.

Aristotle's concept of happiness is tied to virtue. People need to be virtuous rather than just leaving their lives to chance. Virtue is subjective and is believed to be an in-between of two extreme ends of human behaviors. Actions can be judged from a negative or positive point of view. All decisions taken by the individual must result from the rational and deliberate actions of the executioner. Therefore, Aristotle outlines the virtues and vices from which one must identify the relevant virtues for a good life. For a happy life, one must incorporate many virtues. The three main components of happiness include life satisfaction, low levels of adverse effects, positive effects, and satisfaction with essential aspects of life. One of the most important aspects of the goal of *eudaimonia* is friendship (Delhey and Steckermeier 2016). Aristotle valued friendship so highly that he thought it was a combination of both pleasure and virtue. Therefore, achieving the perfect self, according to Aristotle, entailed rational reflection.

Differences between Plato and Aristotle's Concepts of Good Life

Plato and Aristotle are regarded as two of the greatest philosophers. Plato, a teacher of Alexander the Great, doubled up as a teacher to Aristotle. Despite their long-lasting relationship as student and teacher, Aristotle later came on to become one of the greatest critics of Plato's theories. Regardless of the criticism, Plato's school of thought influenced Aristotle greatly. Some of the things they agreed on included the idea that knowledge was absolute and unchanging. The concept of living a good life was discussed by both greats, with Socrates chipping in on some of the wisdom. Their concepts of the good life have been subject to philosophical discussions generations after their time.

Plato

Plato's school of thought is difficult to challenge. He was Alexander the Great's teacher and has been known for his contribution in different fields—physics, astronomy, philosophy, and many other knowledge areas. Plato discussed a good life from a unique perspective. According to Plato, every person has an equal opportunity to live a good life. There are no limitations to who can live a good life and who is limited. By implying that everyone has an equal opportunity to a good life, we can already derive that Plato did not attach the value of a good life to material possession (Carr 2014). Had he thought in the line of wealth and power, the opportunities would not be equal. There are people born rich, others languishing in poverty. Regardless of a person's state, Plato taught that the decision to live a good life was based on one's desire.

To live a good life, Plato put it plainly that one had to move out of their "cave" and venture out to the world. From this view, we understand that Plato emphasized how exposure to the outside world played an essential role in living a good life. Therefore, a good life is one where the person has had experiences with other issues, people, and events other than self. This line of thought is supported by Socrates, who taught that a good life entailed no doing the routine activities every day. Digging deeper into Plato's work and finding that every person, animal, or even tool has a natural function. When the natural function is fulfilled, then that can be termed as a good life. A good life was not just tied down to human beings. Primarily, a chair is meant to be sat on. If the chair serves its purpose, then that is a good life. In human beings, these natural functions determine the quality of lives that we lead.

To understand a human being's natural functions, Plato broke down the human soul into three parts: the intellect, spirit, and physical. All these three have different needs that must be fulfilled to merit the standards of a good life. The intellect gets replenished by knowledge, truth, reality, and understanding; the spiritual and physical gets replenished differently. For a person to lead a good life, all three parts must receive nourishment. If the physical gets replenished at the intellect's expense, it cannot get termed a good life. According to Plato, to lead a good life, one has to balance the parts of the soul's needs. Plato's philosophy applies to all things, living and non-living.

Aristotle

The long-serving student of Plato was not shy of criticizing some of the teachings of Plato. Unlike Plato's teaching, where the school of thought applies to people, animals, and tools, Aristotle focuses more on the people. According to Aristotle's teaching about a good life, he says that everyone is after happiness. The achievement of happiness is the goal that dictates whether a person has lived a good life or not. The pursuit of happiness is a quest for everyone, but whether we get to achieve it or not is not conclusive. Aristotle already paints a different image from that which Plato had suggested. Happiness is a subjective feeling. People derive happiness from different things. While others are happy with social recognition, others may want money and power. Happiness, therefore, has no standard measure (Marmodoro 2014). This school of thought is about the ends and means. While setting out to pursue a good life, the eyes get fixed on a price—happiness. Aristotle describes a good life in three different scenarios. To lead a good life, one has to accumulate possessions that make them happy. These possessions are in the forms of goods—bodily, external, and goods of the soul. The bodily goods are those of pleasure and health, external are food and drinks, and the soul includes knowledge, love, skills, and other intangible qualities.

The acquisition and development of good habits are facilitators of a good life. Virtues such as courage, justice, and moderation are the fundamental teachings of Aristotle. These are virtues that should be cultivated over time and maintained once a person masters them. Besides these three significant virtues, Aristotle taught that a good life gets accomplished when one understands the importance of generosity, friendship, temperament, discretion, and truthfulness. He said that these virtues get cultivated like a good fruit; they take time to nurture. The last consideration, according to Aristotle, is an element of good luck. Human beings require good luck to lead a good life.

The teachings of the teacher and pupil are diverse in some areas. However, there are areas where understanding shows about leading a good life. The idea that a balance must get reached between the physical, intellect, and soul is seen in both concepts. Aristotle and Plato understood that a good life strikes a perfect balance between the satisfaction of these unique needs. We know from their schools of thought that leading a good life is not about the material possession that one possesses. The physical alone is just a component of a trio that must be accomplished. From my philosophical understanding, living a good life is the self-actualization that is arrived at when a person is confident that they have done their best to be a version of themselves that makes them proud.

Ancient Philosophy and the Concept of a Good Life.

Through the provision of the ancient philosophers, there are various rules for being happy and attaining every human life's highest goal. Even though most of these philosophers disagree on the fundamental definition of happiness, they both agree on the various steps to achieving happiness. Also, most of these philosophers from Socrates recognize the importance of happiness in living a good life. Therefore, in the philosophical work of ancient Greeks like Aristotle, we come up with the best way to treat people, eliminate worry, and handle liberty in our modern society. Aristotle's virtues for happiness remain even in today's cancel culture.

Courage

In section six of his third book, *The Nicomachean Ethics,* Aristotle discusses courage, which is the first moral virtue. According to the philosopher, courage is often confused with impulsive risk-taking. The two do not, by any chance, stand as a substitute for the other. Courage is seen as the absence of fear. They can do what has to be done without hesitating.

An example that he gives is the courage of a soldier that goes to war. They, without doubt, face the fear of death but still relentlessly push the enemy. That is courage, not needless risk-taking. Impulsiveness may at times lead to one making rush decisions that are in the pretense of courage. Aristotle's view of courage is relevant to date (Carr 2014). Courage is the balance between recklessness and cowardice. Both extremes are discouraged by Aristotle. When one is cowardly, they are afraid of making moves based on fear of the unknown. A coward will tread extra cautiously, and that will cause them to miss out on opportunities. An excessively reckless person may find themselves being overambitious in their actions.

In the present day, there is a lot of relevance associated with the elements discussed by Aristotle in courage. We are faced with numerous scenarios where one must choose between how to deal. With the introduction of modern issues like the money economy, technology, and other fluctuating factors, risks have become more diverse. The diversity of these risks means that people need to find a balance between risk-taking and cowardice. Take an example of a stockbroker; they must deal in a stock market where prices follow the random-walk theory. Excessive risk-taking is no more than gambling. On the other hand, doing nothing means your hands are tied, and you may fail to deliver on expectations. By following Aristotle's teaching, it is possible to understand the necessity of balancing the two concepts. This could as well be related to taking calculated risks based on an informed point of view.

Courage, and not excessive risk-taking, or cowardice can help one lead a good life. It gives one the flexibility to avoid making decisions from a subjective point of view. The balance between cowardice and recklessness means one can gauge where they are and the available options. When accompanied by critical thinking, courage reduces the possibility of one being too afraid to act even when they know the decision is the right one to go. If the conditions are right, a person must act before they lose their advantage in whichever field. An example of a student in the present day, panic and fear during examinations could cause them to forget the answers to questions they have already studied. When they gain courage, it boosts their confidence and allows them to tackle difficult questions with prior knowledge. Courage, therefore, assures a person that even when they are faced with difficult situations, they may still be capable of working through the situations they are in.

Self-Control

Self-control, according to Aristotle in *The Nicomachean Ethics*, is a virtue that every person must possess. It involves knowing the right thing, making the decision, and being assertive enough to stick to the decision they have made. Aristotle describes self-control as understanding the right thing and following up on the decision made to ensure that the decision maker sticks the right decision that has been made in the long run. There is an element of assertiveness that Aristotle implies but does not express directly in context. Self-control applies to several things in life. The ability to resist temptations is what the philosopher dwells on. In our daily lives, there are a lot of temptations that arise. These temptations are often in line with the selfish needs of individuals. To look past their self-indulgence and selfishness, they are in a position to resist their desires. When presented with an opportunity to choose, some people would stick to their stubbornness and make decisions that are not controlled. This rush has negative consequences in return.

In modern day, countless scenarios call for one to practice self-control. Which we all know is just not easy. They are making an example of public office holders who are entrusted with resources for the public's good. Okay, well we know better, but the idea is there! These people are expected to work with what they are entrusted with to improve those in the community. The temptation to pocket these resources may be great, but self-control will remind the individual of their duty to others ahead of themselves. Self-indulgence pushes people into actions that are beyond what they would typically do. A good example is a gluttony. Gluttony is considered a lack of self-control because one forces themselves to consume more than they need. These are some of the incidents that Aristotle factors in when warning against falling into temptation.

Self-control improves the quality of life that we lead in these modern times. Self-control has an effect of building confidence and trust that other people show in you. Once they identify that a person has self-control, they are trusted with more responsibility and resources. It is a virtue that most employers look to instill in their workforce. A person that practices self-control will not be subjected to excessive scrutiny. They are allowed autonomy or independence. This freedom given based on your ability to control your desires goes a long way in building a person's confidence and morale. Some of the temptations that come our way, like being spendthrift, may be temporary satisfaction but have adverse long-term effects. Therefore, by refusing to indulge in these desires, a person saves themselves the pressure of compensating for bad mistakes made at the moment. Aristotle's understanding of self-control is relevant in the present day. The warnings against self-indulgence and selfishness show us that we should factor in the effects on other people when making choices. Self-control is an intrinsic regulatory mechanism. The ability to withhold temporary satisfactions for long-term benefit is the ultimate show of self-control.

Generosity

Aristotle discusses generosity as his third virtue in the book *The Nicomachean Ethics*. Generosity is a balance between stinginess and wastefulness. A stingy person will not be readily willing to share what they have. A wasteful person does not use what they have responsibly; they are always looking to give and spend without consideration. The philosopher explains that generosity is not determined by the amount given but the habit of the giver. Giving everything you own is not generosity; it is wastefulness. Generosity begins with the ability to take care of what you have and avoid excessive usage. Once you have taken care of that in your possession, it puts you in a position to help others. Aristotle warns against wastefulness because it depleted the resources of an individual. Similarly, a wasteful person often finds themselves prey for people who want to take advantage of their generosity. A generous person must strike a balance between wastefulness and stinginess. They must understand the art of giving to the right person, the right amount, and at the right time.

In the modern day, there are a lot of people who practice active philanthropy. Remember, when I spoke of a hobby earlier; mine just so happens to be a philanthropy, and it has truly changed my life for the better. Philanthropy involves the promotion of the welfare of others through the generous donation of money, time, and other material. Philanthropy is the modern-day show of the virtue that Aristotle promotes. While philanthropy often involves large donations, it is crucial to understand that the amount does not matter. A person who gives regularly is better than one who gives bulk, once. One who gives time and energy is also important to philanthropic goals. Generosity involves sharing that which we have with those who are in need. There have been many lessons from the likes of Mahatma Gandhi and Mother Teresa that has emphasized the virtue of giving. These are all complimentary teaching to what Aristotle taught. When we are in a position to help, we should be of assistance. However, when helping others, we must be careful not to spend more than our means. We have a duty to ourselves before any other person.

Generosity is a virtue that helps us lead better lives. Helping others earns us respect, friendships, and loyalty. While these three are important aspects, there is also the satisfaction that helping others brings. Generosity ensures that whatever we have, we share with others, and in return, when we are in need, we are likely to get help. Human beings are said to be social beings. We live best when helping each other get to the positions we want. No one person is on an island; everyone needs help at one point. Generosity teaches us the importance of considering the needs of others.

Through the philosopher's teaching, we understand that the first thing is taking care of what we have. Once we take care of our possession, it puts us in an excellent position to help ourselves and others. In addition to what Aristotle teaches, we come to understand that the culture of giving should be a continuous habit. Whether we have plenty or less, generosity is about the act, not the amount given. While striving to be generous, we must be careful not be get exploited. There are people who take advantage of generosity and confuse it for weakness.

Friendliness and Politeness

Aristotle places friendliness and politeness as a virtue even though some may argue about its qualification as a virtue. Friendships are essential because human beings are social beings. Without friendliness and politeness, we are not complete. In support of Aristotle's teaching of friendship, there are supporting teachings like that of Abraham Maslow. Maslow's theory classifies social needs as the need to belong. Similarly, Aristotle insists that we should be friendly and polite, without being too friendly. Just as with the other virtues, there is a need for a balance in this virtue. Aristotle refers to friendship as two souls within one body, meaning the bond should be intensely cultivated and impossible to break. One of the most potent convictions from the philosopher's teachings is that friendship is like a ripening fruit; it takes time to mature. In true friendship, there is no need for justice or intervention. Friendliness and politeness are a pillar for finding common ground to tread on. There is a lot of emphasis on the importance of these two concepts for human benefit from Aristotle's teachings. Further in his teachings, Aristotle explains that friendliness is based on utility, pleasure, and goodness. Utility refers to the mutual benefit derived by the parties from the friendship. Pleasure is in terms of the enjoyment of the company, looks, and traits that friends appreciate from one another. Goodness is friendship based on the nature of the people's kindness and cares for each other's welfare.

In modern day, friendliness and politeness are valued and taught in schools as etiquette and courteous behavior. In workplaces, learning institutions, social places, and any other setting that involves interaction with others, everyone must be friendly and polite. It makes human interaction more bearable and accommodating. Where there is friendliness, conflict is less likely to arise. Even when conflict arises, there is a high probability that a solution will be found promptly. Aristotle's teachings on friendliness are relevant to date. It is essential to understand the basis of friendship, whether it is because of utility, goodness, or pleasure. By understanding the foundations of friendship, it becomes increasingly possible to maintain a friendship. Similarly, good friendships are grown over time. Through Aristotle's teachings, we are aware of the importance of establishing these relationships procedurally and over a period. Politeness has a positive correlation with friendliness. People tend to find polite people to be more welcoming than others. Being friendly is virtuous, but some people get uncomfortable when we become too friendly.

In our present lives, politeness and friendliness are appreciated in society. Friendly people tend to have their way in the world because they are easier to help. They cultivate a feeling of warmth around them, such that it does not appear bothersome to interact with them. Politeness earns admiration and respect from society. All this combined plays a role in improving the charisma that one possesses. Politeness and friendliness make an individual easy to work with. As a result, they are not shunned but embraced and praised in society.

Tact and Discretion

In the book *The Nicomachean Ethics*, Aristotle teaches on the need to value the virtue of being procedural and not getting carried away. Tact and discretion involve being procedural and keeping information on a need-to-know basis. In a way, Aristotle teaches against pride. Pride goes against the principles of discretion. Once one is proud, they cannot keep information to themselves; they share information that should be kept silent. Based on rush actions that are not coordinated, there is a high possibility of failure that lacks tact and discretion. Tact is about the evaluation of the when and how. The time to act must be definitive; the manner must be absolute. From what Aristotle teaches, it is easier to achieve the desired goals when one acts within their limits to meet the required objectives.

Aristotle's teachings on tact and discretion are virtues that are present even in modern-day livelihood. There are so many projects, plans, and objectives that we set out to accomplish. Take an example of a project manager who organizes the resources allocated to achieve organization objectives; how the manager proceeds will dictate whether the project will be successful or not. The teachings of Aristotle will advise the manager to be tactful in their operations. If there is work to be divided, additional resources needed, and other considerations, it must be done in advance before the project proceeds further. These are some of the minor details that need greater attention. Issues should be addressed immediately as they arise and with the considerations of virtuous operations. Discretion also applies to reduce the damage caused by the progress of a project because of external interference. When planning, it is advisable not to disclose all the details because it may hinder progress. By keeping people less informed, it gives you the power to control how things unfold. You become the author of the narrative.

Tact refers to the skill and sensitivity of an individual when dealing with others under different circumstances. In contrast, discretion refers to the quality of behaving or speaking to avoid important information or offend others. In daily life, an individual interacts with different people, and this skill is needed to handle different people. Aristotle states that individuals should listen to what they should and say what they should say. The kind people one speaks or listens to makes a difference in one life (Marmodoro 2014).

Additionally, Aristotle claims that there is a deficiency with reference to the mean of how an individual speaks or listens to others. Some individuals carry excess humor when talking or listening to others. These individuals are referred to as vulgar buffoons by Aristotle. Vulgar buffoon individuals are obsessed with jokes and thus, like listening to individuals who make many jokes or like making excess jokes to others when talking to them. These individuals avoid pain at all costs in exchange for fun since they enjoy extra laughter whatever they go. Additionally, Aristotle classified individuals who neither like making jokes nor listening to jokes as boorish and unpolished. These individuals are always severe and take every subject in the discussion as a serious matter, and thus they do not waste their time listening to jokes even when it is leisure time. They take life seriously and expect individuals who are talking to them to take life seriously since they do not entertain humor in their discussions (Tachibana 2018). Aristotle went ahead and classified individuals who joke and listen to jokes moderately as ready-wit. These individuals understand when it is time for making jokes and time for serious business. These individuals change with situations since they know when it is time for making jokes and time for serious business. Additionally, they understand how to pass information to other individuals depending on the situation. They give serious information with the seriousness it deserves and understands where to make jokes.

To this middle stage, ready-wit belongs to the individual and sensitive tact when dealing with other individuals. A tactful individual will not listen to all kinds of jokes since they understand that individuals are not the same. There are some words that an individual can make which can offend other people. Additionally, this individual will not make jokes with terms that lawgivers prohibit. It means that a tactful person will be ethical and thus will follow the laws of the nations and moral norms that control good behavior in the society. Tactful individuals are peacemakers with everyone since they understand the surroundings and individuals interacting with them.

Therefore, Aristotle advocated that it is essential for individuals to be tactful to interact with society well. Just individuals will live a good life in the community since they can interact will other individuals without offending them. They understand what to say, to who, and at what time. Additionally, they do not listen to everything that other individuals are being told since they avoid listening to things that will offend them. These individuals talk and listen to morally good things. They live a good life in society while at the same time living a moral life.

Tact and discretion are the epitome of privacy and preparedness; they can improve the quality of life that we lead. By being tactful, an individual minimizes the risks that they expose themselves to. You will be more ready to deal with situations, but nothing catches you unawares. You are always informed of the situation around you, and it allows you to prioritize how and what to handle first. This preparedness manner is relevant, especially when dealing in fields exposed to high levels of risks. Discretion is privacy and confidentiality. It is commonly said that what people do not know, they cannot destroy. Therefore, in these present times where media, especially social media, covers so much, we must keep as much to ourselves as possible. It exposes us to less damage with our information out in the public domain. Aristotle's teachings have withstood time and changes in the society because they are based on virtues that are absolute. While issues like ethics and morality may be subjective, virtues remain constant despite the times. By being careful in how we operate, it improves the ability to achieve more success.

Aristotle on Friendship and Politeness

While Aristotle wrote on different disciplines, his contribution to friendship cannot be underestimated since his observation on friendship more than 2000 years ago applies up to date. Aristotle observed that one of the real joys of life is friendship and stated that they must have had real, meaningful, and lasting friendships for individuals to claim that they once well lived. Aristotle claims that friendship is a source of joy for all individuals, including extremely rich and absolutely poor individuals. Friendship is a core, and thus every individual must interact with other individuals in their daily activities to enjoy life (Tachibana 2018). Friendship begins at a tender age where individuals correct the young ones from error to the aged by taking care of the aged who cannot perform some of their duties. Aristotle claims that true friendship exists where individuals come together with a common purpose. To date, Aristotle's observations hold since a true friendship has been observed where individuals take care of the aged and young individuals. Individuals in modern society struggle to live a legacy and claim they well lived by at least reaching and assisting others regardless of their financial status. In helping others, people will live an extraordinary life while practicing moral norms in society.

Aristotle outlined a type of friendship that exists among individuals that is more accidental than intentional. He claimed that individuals become friends without their notice, and they end up having a powerful bond. He classified this type of friendship as a friendship of utility. In this friendship, individuals become friends not because of affection but because of the benefits they receive from one another. When the services each gets from the other ends, then the friendship ends too. This kind of company is common in today's society since people become friends in learning institutions when assisting one another in course work. Still, their friendship ends when they do away with their studies. Aristotle predicted today's society accurately. In the friendship of utility, individuals are there to benefit one another and thus promote ethical behavior since these friends are there for one other. At the same time, each party takes care of hurting one another, as observed by friends of utility in the workplace in modern society.

Additionally, Aristotle observed a friendship based on mutual appreciation as the best type of friendship since one individual appreciated the other individual's virtues dearly. In this type of friendship, individuals are attracted to one another based on the virtues they own. Individuals with high integrity levels get attracted and become friends with other individuals who also display high integrity levels. In this friendship, Aristotle observed that individuals remain bonded together despite challenges they may face together. They are together during the worst and the best moments since they share ordinary virtues.

Additionally, respect for one another is the guiding principle for these friendships. If individuals respect one another when in friendship, they will gain joy in spending time with one another and thus live a good life since they will have mental and emotional health. These individuals, since they respect one another, maintain ethical standards while living a good life. Aristotle stated that individuals should invest in friendship since they cannot claim that they lived a good life if they had no healthy and reliable companionship. In modern society, true friendship has been observed among different individuals where individuals have been able to undertake business deals together and thus benefitting one another. Additionally, people have gotten into partnership business where they maintain ethical standards in their production. These individuals in partnership business live a good life since they get income from their company while at the same tie maintaining ethical standards. Indeed, individuals can live a good life and ethically.

The Virtue of Truthfulness and Integrity

Aristotle places truthfulness between vices of habitual lying and being boastful. Truth is the conformity of intellect, and therefore, knowing conformity is knowing the truth. Aristotle stipulates that the virtue of truthfulness is discovered and built-in an individual life. Aristotle defines integrity as the virtue of practicing and doing what one believes in. These virtues by Aristotle are still essential and applicable in modern society. The truthfulness virtue is independent of culture as what is real remains so to everyone, everywhere, and at all times. People, in all places and at all times, will recognize truth as an essential virtue. Aristotle believed that what one believes in cannot change the fact regardless of the belief's sincerity. In modern society, truth is considered as a function of one's culture and the surrounding environment.

Integrity is an essential virtue in modern society. Integrity helps an individual grow in morality and hence contributes to a better life. Integrity allows one to do according to own beliefs and increases competence abilities, contributing to reasoning and living own life. This leads to a peaceful society as people live in harmony and with a great understanding of each other. Integrity also helps individuals learn how to live with others. From one belief's, people will be able to predict different reasonings and actions and better social coexistence in society. Therefore, the virtue of integrity is essential in modern society as it enables people to live with peace, harmony, trust, and understanding (Carr 2014). The virtue of faithfulness requires us to state things as they are without an outside influence that would lead to us making an understatement or overstatement of a particular fact. Aristotle motivated us never to be worried about offending people with the truth. The virtue of truth is the foundation of justice in modern society. Truthfulness helps improve and grow the character of an individual. Honesty is a virtue that contributes significantly to the success of individuals and society as a whole. Truthfulness also helps one live a peaceful and happy life as he does what he believes is right and proper (Carr 2014). Truth is a virtue that also raises an individual's confidence level and helps people do things without fear. Truthfulness is, therefore, a fundamental virtue in society. Being truthful also helps individuals obtain a sense of self-understanding and discover their weaknesses and strengths; all that makes them happy. The virtue of truthfulness helps people learn how to present themselves according to their reputation and all they believe. Truthfulness and integrity, therefore, help people achieve their set goals and commitments on time. This helps create a better understanding of society and success, as everyone has a sense of responsibility.

Aristotle's virtue of truthfulness and integrity is very applicable in modern society as it contributes to a better social coexistence among the people in the community. Honesty and integrity also help individuals grow in character and have better lives. Additionally, if people in society will practice truth and integrity in their daily life, they will make life better since these two virtues play an essential role in human interactions. These virtues are per existing norms in society, and hence individuals can live a good life while keeping the ethical standards as per current moral norms in the community.

Aristotle on Good Temper

According to Aristotle, good temper refers to anger. Individuals with good temper are not extremely angered or deficiently angered. An individual who gets tempered with the right things, at the right place, and with the right people is praised for having good tempers (Gross 2006). A good-tempered individual does not get angered by small things. Individuals know how to control tempers. This individual does not get angered for a long period because the individual has mechanisms to cope with and control extreme anger. A good-tempered individual, as per Aristotle, is not revengeful but gives allowance for forgiveness. Those individuals who do not get angry with things they are supposed to be angry with are considered fools because they do not feel things that should have pained them. Additionally, these individuals are considered fools because they do not defend themselves when wronged, which should not be Aristotle's human beings' nature.

Excess anger is witnessed when an individual gets angry with the wrong person, with the wrong things. These individuals get angered too quickly and for a long time. Aristotle observed another group of people who he classified as hot-tempered individuals (Tachibana 2018). They get angered by the wrong things, wrong people, and quickly. The best thing about hot-tempered individuals is that their anger ceases quickly. Their anger ends immediately because they openly display their anger when wronged, and thus, after expressing their anger, their tempers come down.

Again, Aristotle observed another group of individuals he called the sulky people. They get angry about the wrong things or people. Additionally, they get angry quickly and for a long time. These individuals remain angered until they get revenge. These are known for causing trouble with friends since they like engaging in fights and punishing individuals who wrong them. These individuals do not know the importance of forgiveness since they only see revenge as the only reasonable alternative to their anger.

Everybody gets angry regardless of the age, gender, race, or social class of the individual. Aristotle advocates that individuals should control their tempers to ensure that they do not have extreme anger cases, leading them into fights and other unethical behaviors. Bad-tempered individuals are worse to live with since they cannot solve their peace issues, for they only think of mechanisms to use to revenge for whatever they have been done. However, individuals can be revengeful but in an ethical manner. People tend to praise individuals who have deficiencies in tempers since they do not get angry. This is misleading because a normal human being should become angry and revenge for self-defense. What matters is how to revenge when we became angry.

Thus, an individual can live in peace with other people in society despite little misunderstandings since they control anger whenever wronged. Individuals can learn peaceful measures to take revenge whenever other people wrong them. This will ensure that people live a good life in society without fights and continuous misunderstandings while at the same time living ethically. One should not claim to have lived a good life if it was challenging to control tempers. In modern society, individuals have been educated on good tempers to prevent common disputes, especially after national elections in different countries. Individuals have learned to control their tempers even when their preferred candidates do not win their elections, leading a wonderful life in a society governed by moral norms. People can live good live ad ethically.

The Virtue of Fairness

Aristotle describes the virtue of fairness as correlated with justice. Fairness involves knowing and being able to treat others better with kindness and respect. Fairness also teaches us to take care of others and always place ourselves in the conditions and situations of life as others as we are all human. Aristotle's virtue of fairness is still applicable in modern society as people will always compare themselves with others. Fairness has great importance in people's lives and society as a whole (Tachibana 2018). It helps people and society, in general, act on the greater good to impact other people in society. This makes it easy for people to live together, with each taking care of the other. Fairness also helps individuals to acknowledge each other's contributions and inputs in general to the society without judging.

This study established that fairness and the ability to take care of others improves our own ways of life. Fairness helps individuals create and build better relations among the people in the society as they support each other. This is important in the community as it leads to a general growth in society's welfare, as a whole. Fairness as a virtue helps people understand that one cannot live entirely by oneself and will need help in life stages. This creates a give-take relationship in the society and hence a better society.

The virtue of fairness also helps us promote happiness among ourselves, promoted by good relations with those surrounding us. This helps reduce the possible vices of people living together, such as wars, hate, and theft. This is possible as people live to protect others and their properties. The virtue of fairness also contributes to the highest need for people to share both materials and thoughts to help each other in society. This improves everyone in the community for better and hence a better coexistence in society. According to Curzer (2012), children as young as three years old understand the act of sharing and its impact on the general levels of happiness. One's happiness is closely tied to the level of satisfaction of the people around them, therefore leading to a happy society.

Fairness also improves individuals' ability to have self-control in their day-to-day lives, become resilient, and better understand and judge situations as they live with others. Therefore, fairness is an essential part of our lives, and we should ensure it is part of our character and moral values as we live with others in society (Curzer 2012). Therefore, people's actions in the community should be guided by treating each bother equally; otherwise, treating others any differently should always be justified. However, Aristotle encouraged us that the fairness principle should be the first to consider in comparing others with ourselves but should not be the only criterion to use.

Therefore, the virtue of fairness should be everyone's moral value as it leads to the improvement of society as a whole. People in the community must take care of each other and treat them with respect, love, and kindness. Fairness is a moral obligation to all individuals in society, and thus it will improve the state of individuals' lives. Everyone should know the virtue of righteousness for a better community.

The Rules of Living a Happy Life

Drawing from the teachings of Aristotle and the other ancient philosopher, Michale Soupis argues that the first step to being happy is examining your life and striving to obtain higher pleasures every time. According to Aristotle, unexamined action would hardly lead to happiness because everything is about planning. Reason is nature's greatest gift to humanity. Apart from physical and mental health, Aristotelian ethics emphasizes the importance of examining our lives and obtaining the greatest need of all times—happiness. A human being must take part in every aspect of their lives. Today, the society has been transformed by changes in technology. The impacts of social media are slowly creeping, but the world must always be part of their decisions.

Secondly, individuals should worry about things within their control and those that they can influence directly. According to various ancient philosophers, the mind and the soul are very crucial to any person's life. The first step to psychological health is minimizing our worries and developing a positive mentality. In this regard, people should worry about those aspects of their lives that they can directly influence. Aristotle affirms this perception through his categorization of the virtues. According to *Nicomachean Ethics*, there are acquired virtues that differ from one person to another and natural virtues common to everyone. The acquired virtues could significantly impact the belief in a natural order of doing things. Aristotle believes that the difference among individuals leads to various perceptions of happiness and a good life. However, human beings must develop the right mentality and approach to adversity. The soul is very important in the overall development of mental health. In modern society, there are various avenues for exposing ourselves to torture and undue stress. Therefore, we should control our responses and maintain a purposeful and flourishing life.

It is also crucial to value social connection and the reciprocal attachment that fill the need for affiliation. One of the distinguishing features of human beings is their unique social instinct. Like Socrates and Plato, Aristotle believed that the need to form a society goes beyond the bare contractual arrangement. The need for friendship is unique among human beings who appreciate the fact that such connections are vital for their living. Aristotle emphasized the importance of associative bonds in achieving a good life. Therefore, the virtue of friendship forms a great pillar in Aristotelian ethics and the idea of living a good life. In modern societies, a genuine connection is diminishing as people spend a lot of time trying to connect with strangers on social media. It's essential to embrace the Aristotelian principle and establish a real connection with true friends.

The fourth principle is seeking peace of mind through calming but true pleasures. People need to go for real happiness. True pleasures are consistent and restrained. In modern societies, the distinction between true and unrealistic need is diminishing. The lives in social media are changing our normal and creating a more virtual lifestyle with limited possibilities. Everyone should identify that the ultimate goal of human is happiness which can only be achieved by setting ethical and realistic goals. Additionally, people should refrain from activities or external forces that negatively impact their thoughts and actions. People require various virtues to live a fulfilling life. Even though the virtues are essential, people may not have all of them. Therefore, people should concentrate only on what useful for their personality. According to Aristotle, psychological health is very important in living a good life because the mind and the soul are one thing. Personal freedom is very crucial as long as their moral compass guides an individual's actions. Therefore, mastering oneself is very important for their psychological and physical development. Philosophy has established a great connection between mental and physical connections.

The sixth principle of living a good and happy life is ensuring balance and harmony in one's endeavors. Aristotle was a champion for moderation. *Nicomachean Ethics* acknowledges the importance of bodily needs like food, alcohol, and sex. However, Aristotle holds that such pleasures can only be good to the soul if pursued with moderation. Therefore, a life properly lived should encompass many cautiously undertaken decisions, for even good things can become harmful if pursued without self-restraint or moderation (Young 2017). When people surpass the limit of a reasonable mean, the outcome may become catastrophic, making the life worthless or impossible to live. Therefore, caution is very important in both ancient and modern societies. We live in an era where we can obtain everything at the touch of a button. Therefore, it is essential to arm ourselves with the highest level of self-discipline to guide our decision-making.

Furthermore, responsibility is the greatest is a crucial aspect of every human life, and everyone should strive to emulate their ways of thinking (Young 2017). Individuals should develop the highest level of self-discipline and be willing to handle their problems without blame-switching thoughtfully. Living a good life is not about making mistakes but owning our flaws and accepting that humans are prone to mistakes. The greatest virtue is the ability to honestly assess one's life and hold yourself accountable for your mistakes. It is not about punishing yourself but ensuring that you understand your contribution to the problem. The first step to solving any problem is identifying the solution. Individuals hardly get themselves in situations beyond their control if they exercise restraint and self-caution, as stated by Aristotle. Blame switching and self-exemption have serious consequences in developing the right moral compass expected for every human being. Exonerating fiction is harmful to the development of a moral compass.

Additionally, prosperity is not the definition of a good life. Prosperity can be viewed differently by different people, and the most common metric is the financial aspects. However, wealth is not always a sufficient measure of a good life or happiness. The poor are not happiest, either, but focused on the financial aspect of life alone. Another dimension of prosperity is through the accumulation of power. We have witnessed many powerful but unwise rulers in the history of the world. Therefore, the virtue of knowledge is very important in living a good life. Aristotle advocates for a balanced approach to life. In this sense, people should strive to accumulate a reasonable proportion of every necessary goods and deed. Wisdom is key to a successful and flourishing life.

Another important principle is always to do good to others and avoid justifying our wrongdoings. Aristotle holds that a good life is just life. Therefore, people should avoid causing injuries to themselves and others (Hoipkemier 2018). Today, society is filled with conflicting messages treating other people. Most people claim that you serve others with the same spoon they serve you. However, even religious teachings are clear that wronging others is a sin. Even though modern societies are very competitive, almost like "man-eat-man societies," individuals should adopt the right moral compass and channel their priorities straight for a just course. It is no secret that people are often ready for vengeance under hard-bitten environments and to harm others, but doing the right thing involves being morally guided. It is very easy to justify malice against others. Some people hide behind the reciprocal notion, while others claim a preemptive gesture in advance of an anticipated injury. Some philosophers hold that the true definition of an individual is what other people say they are. In this regard, how an individual treats other people will significantly determine their image in public.

While most cultures assume that payback is an acceptable response to any situation, there is limited knowledge provided on the effects of perpetrating evil on other people. Even if one does not know it, victimizing others has psychological impacts on the victimizer and thus affects their ability to live a good life (Hoipkemier 2018). Kindness is a virtue that is not only admired but also gives great rewards. Helping other people realize a sense of satisfaction is essential in the quest for a good life. Ancient Greek philosophers examined the positive effects of kindness on the giver. Helping others has various emotional rewards, which are essential in living a good life. Kindness rewards those who show compassion and desire to help others. The value of human connection is the ability to provide a shoulder for others to lean on.

Aristotle argues that all human actions are geared towards achieving happiness. According to Aristotle, happiness is a state in which a person obtains all the good throughout their lifetime. It is, therefore, a state in which an individual has everything that they need and lacks nothing. In this regard, happiness is not a means but an end, thus defining a good life. *Nicomachean Ethics* examines happiness in terms of wealth, friends, temperance, and knowledge, which can help attain the perfection of human nature and even enrich human life. It further provides that one must have certain moral virtues like courage, friendliness, self-control, generosity, tact, and discretion for one to attain the ultimate happiness. When effectively incorporated, these moral virtues will help one to lead a flourishing lifestyle. As discussed above, most of these virtues complement one another, like generosity and friendliness. Aristotelian ethics comprehensively explains the relevance of these virtues in a human's life, showing why physical and mental health alone is not sufficient for a good life.

Using the various moral virtues, Aristotle explains how to live a good life and maintain one's moral compass. Living a virtuous life entails, but is not limited to, generosity and showing kindness to others helps and courage in facing one's troubles. Even though various people have different definitions of a good life, everyone wants to be happy in whichever life they lead. Therefore, happiness is the end for any successful life. Aristotle constructs his argument about a good life by considering the soul and the mind a single element in the human body. From this point, he outlined the relationship between bodily, emotional, and behavioral traits in achieving a good life. Virtue ethics has proven very useful in the contemporary world, where the distinction between good and evil is becoming highly subjective. Using Aristotelian virtues, individuals can improve their behaviors to live a morally upright and fulfilling life.

Okay, so now I would hope you are laughing because of this last portion. I mean, can you imagine a smartass like me telling you that tact is important to your development in life? So, couth may not be my strongest attribute, but you get the jist of it. This is just proving my point from earlier that it is a constant work, and nothing is ever really all sunshine and roses. In fact, I am learning as I go myself. However, herein lies the truth: life is interesting, life is disingenuous, life is hard to understand, and life takes a toll on us all. Is it not funny that the philosophers of so long ago talk about all the things we still have not figured out? They lay out a map with a suggested course yet we, as people, still cannot seem to follow. That is simply because we are human; there is error where there are ideas. We may not understand, and we may never really grasp it. That is what life is, a walk with the philosophers in the cloud of the unknown. However, the teachings they leave us can be that guiding light. We are ever learning and developing our own direction. Life is ours and we live it our way...

CHAPTER 8

AN EPIC FINALE

What is it all about? What is life? What does it entail? What drives humanity? What is the ideal life? What is its point? Where are all these headed to? Why does the sun never stop? How comes there is a lot of perfection and imperfection around? Nothing makes sense around life. But a lot goes around with or without the questions. Does it have a direction? Does it have a bearing? How the get did humanity get down here? Reverse engineering gives a different meaning. On the other hand, philosophy, theology, and all the other basics give twisted meanings that add more complication than purpose.

Okay, this is it, this is heading nowhere, and the entire point aims at giving answers to unending questions, which have little meaning and significance. The truth is no solution provides precise answers to humanity's eternal questions. Life entails many things put together, and understanding the basics is all that matters. But hold on, does the mind have enough capacity to hold all these? No need to go there; little will come forth. Of course, life presents more than humanity can take. In short, the more the questions, the more the confusion. The short end of it all is this: humanity lacks any meaningful answer to all the happenings around humanity.

However, there must stand out something relevant worth noting about life, its reality, significance, and the human experience. Human consciousness remains cloudy. Do not ask about what consciousness is about. It is neither here nor there; maybe some conceived ideology about something that is nonexistent or exists only in mind. Just perhaps, but the truth is there is a lot more about all these that explanation cannot do. The best one out to do is "hold on to the facts." Do not get wise, and do approach it philosophically. The chances of getting lost are higher than winning a lottery. Big questions can make the whole exercise worse. Small questions can complicate things, while not questioning can only make the entire scene look ugly. Live and let live till death do you part with life, forever. Take it lightly; it is not all that serious.

How about an Open Mind?

Forget the questions. Do not dwell on the answers. They mean little or may mislead you. The worst groups of persons to "take a walk with" are the philosophers. They will make you look like Mickey Mouse. We learn so much from them yet understand so little. The critical thing to uphold is an open mind; just do not let the brains fall out. Keeping an open mind is about remaining conscious of life's happenings, diversity, confusion, and all its haste and noise. Some wisdom, eh! But behind such sound wisdom and insight, life will still make "dark" plans behind your back, messing up every good damn act one hard in place. What the heck? Anyway, that is stretching it too far. Life is all about nothing! No, life is all about experience as one makes their way towards their last breath.

Little Choices Made for Us

No one chooses their parents. No one decides anything whether to be born male or female, American or European, Black or White, healthy or ugly, and no one gets to choose where they are born. It all depends on luck. Luck further gives an insight into the absurdity of life again. It all depends on luck! If one is lucky, they get good parents, born in a royal family in the best part of the world, and within one's desired setting. But how can these come about with life's unpredictability? Nothing makes sense, and no one seems to care.

Everyone seems to go with the tide, hoping, praying, and looking forward to the best of Lady Luck. What a sick way to live and come about. Life is all about luck, or maybe it seems. But why would such a magnificent thing be based on a simple thing as luck? Maybe people have not learned how best to get the Lady Luck. Or perhaps people have not known how to increase their chances of luck in life. But how can one increase their chances of uncertainty, yet no one seems to have control, no one seems to know what is going on? First, there are no sure guarantees, and even if even one had the chance to increase their luck, how would they do it without prior education and knowledge about life? I must contend that life is a roll of the dice. But it should not take this direction, and it should not be so.

Laugh Your Way to Get Meaning

First things first, no need to take anything overly serious in life. The best approach to the above unending questions and situation is to approach it through humor. Dropping the hard mentality and approach is the first key to getting meaning to this absurdity. No doubt, it is a comical experience comprising of some serious issues, on top of all is death! It sounds creepy and chilling. Laughter is critical; it is the first antidote to anything that may cause distraction and hinder meaning. Laughing is good, healthy, and enjoyable. Psychologists argue that laughter is medicine. Whether it comes in the form of tabs or injections, they understand better. But laughter has a unique way of getting one along their intricate paths. Laughter is a distraction, and it is a promoter of light moments. Many have held the firm belief that laughter is an effective weapon, especially in the face of difficult moments. Remember earlier that "dark humor is a part of life, accept it"? Yeah, well, time to use it! So mote it be.

Life is all about absurdity. If another layer of absurdity is added to the humorous aspect of life, it is a double dose of confusion and joy. Laughter and humor play a critical role in relieving pressure, held up negative energy, and tension. High anxiety situations tend to bottle things up and increasing mind and body pressure. Laughter is the ultimate answer to pent up anger or stress. Introducing humor to a serious situation is a sign of strength; it commands positions and conditions. Often, people with a good sense of humor have unique ways of overcoming adversities. Arousing humor helps in promoting a positive mood. It is linked to increasing the pleasure and satisfaction of life. Engaging in the very best of life and getting the very best. Humor also plays a critical role in enhancing one's sense of wellness and positivity despite the negativity. It serves as a defense mechanism, a strategy of keeping negativity at bay.

This is getting nowhere, just like the very breath of life. Do people know where they want to get in life? No, really. The chances are high that the majority have little idea about their next course of action. Many have not had the opportunity to explore the world and life. Many are still searching out for the many answers, such as the above poised. However, many have something that interests them, causing them to act in a certain way, pursue a given path, and work hard. Many have a sense of direction where they would like to be in two or three or ten years to come. Many have concepts about how to get there. But a large number have little idea about what is going on. It is all happening under the sun.

At the same time, many do not even know how to live. They flip from day to day with no sense of direction or clue about their future. Just because of the breath of air, they have the energy to get going. Many keep learning, keep going, and keep hoping for that one great break, that one chance that will bring sense and insight into their lives. But one thing is exact amidst all these complex issues—the will power to live against many challenges. Things never happen, and in many instances, things always go against wishes, dreams, and aspirations. Such is the time reality dawns, and things get thicker if not cloudy. Life has the beautiful habit of falling apart the very moment it is expected to make sense. It is like a bad omen, and an intentional setback rolled back to turn around and scorn humanity. And many never have it their way. It is the sad reality behind everything. The only meaningful thing people derive pleasure from is the sense of working towards a goal, an objective, and a meaningful living. In many ways, this is the only thing in life that makes some level of sense. But no one ever has it their way. There is always the wrong side to life in all humanity's efforts, the challenges.

Life's challenges have one common characteristic: they always put a stop to many dreams. Challenges have this common tendency of giving life a bad name. Whether it is part of life or just another terrible omen from another planet, no one knows. Challenges always pop-up at the very moment they are least expected and wanted. Why? No more questions. Get the basics and stop overstretching your mind. The beautiful thing about life is that, in a way, it understands humanity's ways, means, desires, and aspirations. Challenges are like speed governors in a vehicle. Challenges always reduce speed, thus inhibiting growth and success. Why would life be so unfair to have an element that is only good at adding misery and sorrow behind all its beauties?

Often, people pretend to take the regular life route but suddenly realize its absurdities and get back to their real selves. Usually, this is the moment life deals one a hard blow. Individuals often reset themselves back to default settings, retrace their steps, and acknowledge the bittersweet aspect of life. If there is one lesson life has often taught everyone, it is to remain humble and recognize that someone controls the remote. The sad reality is that no one knows and has the power to reset the remote and get things back to their standard settings. Getting mixed up amidst everything further complicates things, but life has a way of reassuring all that the sun will rise and set again as if nothing of significance happened despite everything. Everyone is thus forced to clasp their glorious mess and the challenges they find themselves. However, the significant difference comes in how one embraces and acknowledges the confusion without making things worse. At the same time, however difficult the situation, it is always wise never to take things seriously. Whichever the case, no one has ever gotten out alive. So, the ending really is the same, do you get it? Look at a map, how many roads lead to the same destination stop focusing on just one.

Making Sense of Everything

The best strategy to come to terms with life's absurdity is to make sense out of them by learning. It is wise to seek knowledge, find the right information, and get a better perspective of all these messes. It is also said that experience is the ultimate power in that understanding one can make a good sense of it. This makes all the difference, giving one the capability and knowhow of forging away. One of the most fundamental aspects of knowing involves acknowledging the right information. Accepting the correct information is all about continually setting the fitting route to making the right decisions. Good decisions are born out of good understanding. Nevertheless, bad choices arise out of the need to rush through life without getting to the basis and foundation of its root cause. At times, life is challenging for some people not because it is genuinely perplexing, but because of our own stupidity. Ooh, such a damp way to perceive it. In most cases, most people do not take an active role in their lives, and when they experience bad things, they sit back and think, *Oh, so this is what is happening? Okay.* It is such a weird way to view and take life. Despite its absurdities and confusion, it still has some sense anyway. Whatever it throws around, people should remain wise not to duck but face them as a way of acknowledging its humorous aspect. If perceived and upheld positively, life is one good rollercoaster worth riding along. It is never worth it to lie down after a hard knock. Most people forget the struggles and instead take a nap after a real hard hit. That is a tragic occurrence. The ability to rise after a hard knock is what makes all the difference. No explanation is needed, and it is never rocket science. But the hard tackle comes with the test even before the lesson. That is such an unfair deal.

Find Meaning in Life

Making sense and finding meaning are two different things, so do not get it twisted. Before going overboard on dealing with life challenges, finding the true meaning behind this hullaballoo stuff called life is essential. Life is a real racket, some dark joke that happened while everyone focused on their next big break. Does it sound obnoxious to deal with stuff as misleading as life? No, it is not abhorrent; it is a mistake altogether. It happened while everyone got busy with other issues; maybe even before birth. Getting meaning behind its tragedy is not only nonsensical but also utterly wasteful. No one has ever made sense out of it, not even the great Greek philosophers. We still have not learned from their teachings. It has become a learn and design as you go. Follow the roads that their guide gives us. The most important thing is to get into activities and habits that will deny you the opportunity to sputter and find true meaning to a means to cope and adapt. That is a mindfuck but a worthy-of-your-time fuck.

First, love people, both the good and the bad. Also love those who might wish to shoot you at the slightest opportunity. Ever loved a robber pointing a gun at you? It sounds like complete gibberish, but that's just how witty it gets. Loving others (whatever that means) is all about forgetting that they need that McDonald Chicken McNugget more than you do.

It is about forgetting about your hunger and focusing on the other person's basic needs. Please get back to the closest people, life partners, children, spouse (but it is difficult loving one always on your toe), and friends (the nonsensical group who will see you while they are merry and keep you that way). These people form a close network of "who is who" as far as those who will aid you in way you could not even imagine. So, get them closer!

Next, detox from technological advancements and get the true meaning of being alive (whatever that means it is different for all of us). Get away from the beauty of social media and out into the field (kindly avoid battlefields; they are counterproductive here). Life has never happened in a vacuum, which is what social media and technological gadgets are all about today. Get out and knock other people's brains out! (Not literally, do not be a dumbass!) Get a life. Spend time walking to nowhere, praying (to whatever you believe in), meditating, and develop a grateful attitude. When all is lost, a thankful spirit is all that can move you from point Z back to A. Then follow the simple rules of the wise—thanks, gratefulness, and appreciation.

The above titbits all entail what one can do to others. How about oneself? Get a hobby that wastes time constructively, like playing football or hockey or anything that will cloud the mind from seeing the true uselessness of life. In short, get busy, find joy in simple pleasures like running and hitting a ball. Or pursue an interest such as running for the presidency of a group or function. It is the easiest thing to do; simply read and learn. Learn from how people of power cheated and rose on your naivety to see current world social climate. (No pun intended; it is just current world culture. Mad respect to all.) Getting an interest and a hobby has multiple benefits. First, it gives one something to do; second, it denies one the opportunity to engage in stupid stuff, for example, trying to get a meaning of life's troubles.

Next, go Plato and Aristotle's way. Those boys never stopped learning. No wonder they formed the wisest group to walk planet earth. (Of course, there just may be other planets too with their Plato and Aristotle.) Intellectuals argue that thirteen years of rigorous school life has a way of molding the mind to productivity and usefulness. Although it is really a life-long process, school time plays a critical role in helping one master the basics of getting around things (whatever they are). Also, high academic qualifications have a unique way of augmenting one's self-esteem, thus increased confidence in handling life's challenging jokes. Go beyond the master's degree and acquire the doctorate level, and if there is another level, go for it. Acquire everything possible under the sun in the name of education. Attain all levels. Growing and learning are Siamese twins; they get along like a hamburger and a coke hunger. On a light note, avoid junk food; they are sure tickets back to the dirt.

The planet earth has over a billion places one can visit. Get money and hit the road. Do not die in one place and expect to have lived a worthy life. Traveling helps one gain an in-depth understanding of the entire noise about life beyond breathing oxygen and exhaling carbon dioxide. Go out and see the world, learn a new language, see the other awkward faces besides yours, and above all, connect with the places at a personal level. You may end up dying in one of the many places around the world, but at least you tried. It is far better than dying in one "shit-hole" where you were born and grew up. Different geographical areas have a unique way of adding a few years to one's miserable depleted years before succumbing to life's pressures. Of course, everyone succumbs, so never think you will get out alive. Setting out a "nice" perspective opens up a million ways to deal with injudicious life problems.

Undertaking the above activities will never guarantee one good, stress-free life. But they can help one deal with life's stupidities on a light note. The nuances and complexities of life can deny an honest living soul of a human being derive the best out of this exercise of breathing in and out. Getting meaning does play a significant role in putting everything, including one's lack of understanding, into the right perspective. When one breaks down, it is never about not knowing, but it is about understanding the basics of never remaining down like Santa Claus in a mud ditch. One is thus capable of finding ways around complicated situations wisely and judiciously. Wisdom has many benefits; chief among them is the ability to avoid stupid decisions and lifestyle. Such is the number one approach to a meaningful and fulfilled life. However, it does not mean that a dopey alternative or decision will not get one far, but it can also come in handy, especially in situations that require less common sense.

Getting Over Life Challenges

The first and most important thing in life is to get a sense of humor, whichever way you look at it. Laugh at sickness, laugh at a robber with a loaded gun pointed at your head, laugh at how you reach orgasm, laugh at your death—laugh, laugh, and find a way with life's experiences. Humor has a ridiculous way of lessening the gravity of things. Imagine things and try to get over them on a light note and in the best way possible. Having such an attitude is akin to taking a painkiller before a migraine takes over. You will find relief long before you experience the ailment. By the time it hits your head, you will be more than healed. Not that you will not experience the pain; the difference will be in the attitude. A positive attitude towards a difficult situation is the first antidote towards getting back to default settings and rewinding the clock to its original locales. Just do not do it as an escape strategy; you will be more than disappointed. Challenges have a way with reverse psychology, and you cannot be any wiser. Play within the rules and avoid alternative "cheeky" ways. Above all, keep the faith and positivity; at times, it is all that matters and counts when push comes to shove. Although one should never "push and shove" even in lighthearted moments or easy challenges.

Life is challenging for those who lack humor in their lives. Watching COVID-19, AIDS, hurricanes, earthquakes, and how strangely loved ones can just die can sound inhuman, but humor, it can leaven the hurt and pain. It is all about being fearless and breaking the rules and norms. When one laughs at wrong but okay things, benign harms, and threatening life situations, they change their mindset about the entire situation. The first and most important thing about overcoming challenges is developing a positive approach to existence and occurrences. For example, having a positive attitude while faced with a problematic situation helps reduce stress and tension. Additionally, having a positive approach while facing a difficult situation serves as critical albeit keeping the spirit high, upholding a sense of humankind, and lowering stress levels. Although some positive approaches may sound ill-fitting, they serve the purpose of tolerating the challenge positively. It is a way in which one makes the challenge an integral aspect of their being positive. Positivity at the very things that threaten humanity is a way by which an individual can maintain a sense of hope and meaning amidst calamities.

Tips and Tricks

Nothing is static about life. The entire concept of life comprises all sorts of ups and downs that always keep people from achieving their life goals. At one time, all is fine and going according to plan; the next moment, everything is in chaos, thanks to challenges. In an instant, you under the bus, rolling like a curved ball. Everyone faces their misfortunes but learning to overcome them remains the most important thing. Everyone has a way out of the rat hole and into the normalcy of life. There are a few useful tricks and tips to get going.

Planning—Despite not having an idea about tomorrow, it is vital to have a laid down organized plan for the patterns of one's life. It would be best to undertake a comprehensive assessment of your environment and situation, always bearing in mind the consequences and outcomes.

Understand that everyone is facing and dwelling in the same shithole; the pile's just different. Many, if not everyone, has their low and high moments. Bearing this in mind is enough to give you the strength and positivity to face what life throws at you with confidence and positivity.

Request for Assistance—The world is full of good-hearted people. Find one; and I know it is easier said than done. If it were easy, everyone would just do it. I got real goddamn lucky and found my fiancée. Moral of the story, if I can figure this out, so can you. These are the people who are always available to help in times of need. Surround yourself with the right persons, get them into your inner circle, and let them know when you're down and bitten beyond help. But do not trust every breathing soul with your problem. Be wise and trust a few.

Get down to your fucking feelings:

1. Never mask how you feel.
2. Get down to your inner soul and understand your inner voice, even if it is as coarse as Shrek.
3. Meditate—it will not actually fix anything, but it is good for you to take a mental break.
4. No matter what you do you cannot succumb to cancel culture of these modern times. Accept it and fucking move on.
5. Pray and experience what psychologists call the cathartic and therapeutic experience. It means a lot to your soul. Through feeling and sharing, one can see a difficult situation in a new light.

Accept Support. Ask for help; it takes a bigger person to do so and remind yourself not to be a stubborn asshole. Just accept support. This is a simple and straightforward strategy every breathing soul can practice. People eager to help care a lot and are a manifestation of a higher calling up in the skies. Also, try and help others; it is a whole new therapeutic experience.

Think broad and strategic. Never let fear bog you down. Expand your horizon and have a bigger picture of your abilities and opportunities. This is a sure way of encountering challenges with a positive mentality. Always dream and think big, daring yourself of higher callings. Inculcating a positive mindset is more than acknowledging the realities of life and accepting some of the things life throws our way.

Lastly, *never give up.* Giving up should never form part of your vocabulary. Life we fail at; cope with that and build your life up. Never giving up denotes having the capability of overcoming the challenges life throws your way. Additionally, never giving up denotes never succumbing to situations that may prove unattainable. All these are achievable by working smart, getting things done strategically, organizing your shit, and acknowledging that, at times, life sucks, but this should not mean the end of life.

The above tricks form a critical aspect of preparing and having a positive mindset about challenges and life's ups and downs. The best way to prepare for the above tricks and tips is by following a simple four-method approach.

First, accept and let go of difficult moments. Accepting is critical to letting go of any chances of having in-built fear, anxiety, and stress. Second, it is critical to observe and decide. It is also critical to establish a plan through the entire experience and decide on the best course of action. The third step is facing fears and acting accordingly. One should recognize and outline the fear or challenging situations then come up with the best mitigation approach. Lastly, one needs to practice gratitude. Practicing gratitude is critical towards reframing the mind to accept the challenge, thus triggering the happy and humorous feeling for the present moment. The most critical thing to note through these steps is that dealing with challenges requires a positive attitude, takes time, and requires persistence.

Despite the situation, nothing in life is impossible. Having this belief is essential for practicing and putting in the best measures required responding to the situation appropriately. Above all else, appreciating that nothing lasts forever is the most crucial thing while acknowledging that challenges are temporary situations in life. No matter the gravity, no matter the complexity, it will always pass. If it does not pass, you will pass. Okay, sorry for this, but some challenges kill, and the best you can do is to die in peace and live as a lasting memory to the few who understood your struggles. So, try as much as possible to suffer decently and help others understand your challenging situation. No need to pull faces; after all, all of humanity passes through multiple challenges that eventually make them stronger or kill them. Sad, but that is the world we live in each passing day. However, never give up on even trying. It is the best you can do amidst the challenges. If you die, you die. If you live, you die another day. No way out of the merry-go-round.

Find Happiness for Fuck's Sake

The next step is deriving happiness from life after finding meaning and a sense of its purpose. However, no one has ever found *the* purpose. There simply is not a singular purpose; it differs for each of us. All beings flip from day to day, struggling to make ends meet. By the way, the most outstanding achievement human beings make in their life under the sun is making ends meet and getting their daily bread as if that is all that matters. Despite life's complications, the most critical thing for any individual under the sun is to derive happiness. Some people always maintain an upbeat attitude about life despite the challenges they encounter. Such is one of the essential things in life that can play a crucial role in increasing happiness and finding a solution to the myriad problems they encounter. One can apply and implement these strategies towards increasing their happiness to keep the impact and significance of life challenges at bay. Happiness has a unique way of giving one a purpose and reason to flip from day to day with significant meaning.

Gratitude

1. Be thankful for every day.
2. Maintain a daily journal in which you jot down what you grateful for each day.
3. Derive the best from your gratitude and never take them for granted.

Give back to society. If you are blessed and grateful, pass it on to others. There is more to giving than receiving. Studies show that people who give derive a lot of meaning and sense from their existence, thus increasing their happiness and positivity towards life. In giving, you care, and in caring, you get psychological satisfaction that goes beyond the thank you from the other party. Giving back to others and society is a sure bet and way of appreciating the many blessings and lessening the burden of others' challenges. By caring about others, life has its unique way of caring about you. Never take it for granted.

Laugh every day. The old intellectuals argued that laughter is the best medicine. Try it out; it is indeed the best medicine, even at the point of death. It relieves pressure and brings forth untold mental positives that are beyond the scope of this paper. Psychologists call the hormones endorphins and oxytocin (whatever they mean) released when one laughs and brings forth a nice feeling somewhere in the brain. By the way, what is the difference between brain and mind? Consult and read further. These are some of the things that deem trivial, but are very critical as far as knowledge is concerned. Whatever the difference, try and increase the amount of those two chemicals and your happiness will triple of quad ripple, whichever comes first.

Take time alone. Love yourself through pampering by taking your time to do your "thing." Medicate or take a long walk in the woods. Be careful of wild animals lest you come back minus your life. Taking time brings forth psychological benefits such as reflecting better on your problems and the many breathing benefits in and out. It is a beautiful feeling, keeping count of your breathing, the very activity that keeps you alive. Life is such a lousy accident that happened along the way. Just through breathing in and out, you're alive and can make decisions—no wonder humans have multiple questions about their existence. Little makes sense. However, that is neither here nor there. Let us get to the bottom of this awful stuff called happiness.

Engage in your best love activity. Forget about your career or profession; get down to what you love, even if it is just a hobby, and enjoy. Love is such a beautiful thing; ensure that you love the right things such as people, relaxation and food.

Exercise. Walk around the block and release excess energy and worldly strife. Studies show that people who exercise derive so much good from life than lazy bones who just idle around with little physical activities. Take a long walk to nowhere in the evening and wake up to a lovely stroll with your dog. If you do not have a dog, go side by side with your shadow; it keeps the company up to the last minute of your breath and never leaves until you turn to ashes and dust. Plus, hey, it is less shit to clean up.

Avoid Regrets. Focus on the good things about your past life and let the bad moments die out. After all, who said you're perfect, never to make mistakes? Get over any past mistake with a shrug of the shoulder and let live.

Eat healthily. Studies and scientists affirm that "you are what you eat." Even if you eat garbage, that is you, and the food will define a great deal of your next life—if at all you have any. Nevertheless, stick to healthy eating. Avoid junk food such as fast-food shit; it really will affect you mentally. Those companies make so much money by sending people to their graves earlier than expected. The agony of life is enough for that; let us not pay people to do it for us. Nevertheless, it is a matter of choice. Get the best eating tips from your nearest life coach or whatever you call them to maintain a good healthy life.

Never compare yourself to others. Every dog has its day, and your day is never their day. Keep it about yourself, and avoid comparing your damn crazy life with that of others. Condition and train your mind to pay more attention to yourself. Happiness is one of the best ways to countering life's challenges. Lay a good foundation to deriving the best from its benefits. If you cannot get happiness from your life now, prepare for your happiness in the next life. Maybe you have better chances on the other side than this on planet earth.

Getting over life's challenges is one of the most important things any individual can do under the sun. It is essential to find meaning and sense out of this lousy business called life. Also, it is essential to have in-built mechanisms of overcoming life problems artistically without much ado. Additionally, it is essential to develop strategic ways and skills of overcoming life's problems and challenges. These include appreciating life and remaining upbeat about the daily struggles that give meaning and purpose to life. For without the struggles and challenges, life would no doubt lose its meaning and significance. Human beings get meaning through purpose through these very challenges. It is thus critical to consider them as part of the very life worth living.

Lastly, increase your happiness by putting in place practices and activities that increase your sense of worthiness, such as loving, exercising, eating healthy, and being grateful. Happiness remains one of the most important things you should strive for each day. You will be better placed to counter challenges if you have and grateful each day. A happy attitude has a unique way of influencing the brain towards overcoming challenges. If all fails, maybe you were never meant to live a decent, stress-free life; wait for a chance in the next life, if you will be lucky enough to get there in one-piece. Hell, the mere acceptance of these issues will help. One thing in life we must never let become disabled is our humor, for without it, everything you just read is meaningless. Though it is tough, it is hard, and it feels like life has us all handicapped, fuck it and we move. There is a scene in the classic 1999 movie *American Pie* where the character Stiffler played by Sean Williams Scott grabs his crotch and says, "Eat this," and walks away. Let me end on this note: just be like Stifler—grab that hypothetical crotch of life and say, "Handicap this!"

NOTES AND REFERENCES

Andrews, Frank M., and Stephen B. Withey. 2017. *Social Indicators of Well-Being: Americans' Perceptions of Life Quality.* Springer Science and Business Media. https://books.google.co.ke/books?hl=en&lr=&id=4g7rB-wAAQBAJ&oi=fnd&pg=PA1&dq=importance+of+be-ing+organized+in+life&ots=cgRo0dk1jZ&sig=we-gOysITLDvFHxZJaZpjnQJhcak&redir_esc=y#v=onep-age&q&f=false.

Awino, Zachary Bolo, Martin Ogutu, and Mary Musyoka. 2018. "Work Culture: Stress Management in Reducing Stress and Improving Organizational Performance." *China-USA Business Review* 17 (3): 144-154. doi:10.17265/1537-1514/2018.03.004.

Boerma, Wienke G. W., and Atie van den Brink-Muinen. 2016. "Gender-Related Differences in the Organization and Provision of Services among General Practitioners in Europe: A Signal to Health Care Planners." *Medical Care* 38 (10): 993–1002. https://www.jstor.org/stable/3767982?seq=1.

Carr, David. 2014. "The Human and Educational Significance of Honesty as an Epistemic and Moral Virtue." *Educational Theory* 64 (1): 1–14.

Centers for Disease Control and Prevention. 2019. "Lead in Jobs, Hobbies, or Other Activities." *CDC.* July 30. Accessed January 3, 2020. https://www.cdc.gov/nceh/lead/prevention/sources/jobs-hobbies-activities.htm.

Corley, Kristen. 2016. "The Ugly Truth Behind Why It's So Hard To Let Go Of Toxic Relationships." *ThoughtCatalog.com.* November. Accessed 2020. https://thoughtcatalog.com/kirsten-corley/2016/11/the-ugly-truth-behind-why-its-so-hard-to-let-go-of-toxic-relationships/.

Curzer, Howard J. 2012. *Aristotle and the Virtues.* New York: Oxford University Press.

Delhey, Jan, and Leonie C. Steckermeier. 2016. "The Good Life, Affluence, and Self-Reported Happiness: Introducing the Good Life Index and Debunking Two Popular Myths." *World Development* 88: 50–66.

Ford, Thomas, Brianna Ford, Christie Boxer, and Jacob Armstrong. 2012. "Effect of Humor on State Anxiety and Math Performance." *Humor* 25 (1). Accessed November 24, 2020. doi:10.1515/humor-2012-0004.

Gross, Daniel M. 2006. *The Secret History of Emotion: From Aristotle's Rhetoric to Modern Brain Science.* Chicago and London: University of Chicago Press.

Hoipkemier, Mark. 2018. "Justice, Not Happiness: Aristotle on the Common Good." *Polity* 50 (4): 547–574.

Holt, Alfred. 1878. "Review of the Progress of Steam Shipping during the last Quarter of a Century." *Minutes of the Proceedings of the Institution of Civil Engineers.* 2–11. doi:10.1680/imotp.1878.22485.

Huang, Li, Francesca Gino, and Adam D. Galinsky. 2015. "The Highest Form of Intelligence: Sarcasm Increases Creativity for Both Expressers and Recipients." *Organizational Behavior and Human Decision Processes* 131: 162–177.

Karube, Narumi, Aya Sasaki, Fumika Hondoh, Chiyo Odagiri, Joji Hagii, Satoshi Seino, Minoru Yasujima, and Tomohiro Osanai. 2016. "Quality of Life in Physical and Psychological Health and Social Environment at the Posthospitalization Period in Patients with Stroke." *Journal of Stroke and Cerebrovascular Diseases* 25 (10): 2482–2487. https://www.sciencedirect.com/science/article/abs/pii/S1052305716301410.

Klausen, Søren Harnow, Bryon Martin, Mustafa Cihan Camci, and Sarah Bushey,. 2019. *Perspectives on Happiness: Concepts, Conditions and Consequences.* Brill.

Konch, Manik. 2019. "Aristotle's Notion of Happiness: An Appraisal." *Editorial Board* 8 (10): 77.

Manson, Mark. 2019. *Everything is Fucked: A Book About Hope.* New York: HarperCollins.

Marmodoro, Anna. 2014. *Aristotle on Perceiving Objects.* New York: Oxford University Press.

Martin, R. 1996. "Current Directions in Psychological Science Volume 5, 1996, Index." *Current Directions In Psychological Science* 5 (6): 187–188. doi:10.1111/1467-8721.ep11512432.

Martin, Rod A., and Herbert M. Lefcourt. 1984. "Situational Humor Response Questionnaire: Quantitative Measure of Sense of Humor." *Journal of Personality and Social Psychology* 47 (1): 145–155. doi:10.1037/0022-3514.47.1.145.

McBride, Dawn M., and J. Cooper Cutting. 2016. *Cognitive Psychology: Theory, Process and Methodology.* Chicago, Illinois: Sage Publications.

McFarland, Cathey, and Roger Buehler. 2012. "Negative Moods and the Motivated Remembering of Past Selves: The Role of Implicit Theories of Personal Stability." *Journal Of Personality And Social Psychology* 102 (2): 242–263.

McGraw, A. Peter, and Caleb Warren. 2010. "Benign Violations: Making Immoral Behavior Funny." *Psychological Science* 21 (8): 1141–1149.

Melissa. 2010. "Deconstructing Murphy's Law." *Qrius.* April 17. Accessed November 24, 2020. https://qrius.com/murphys-law-history/.

Morgan, Jessica Kelley, Laurel Hourani, and Stephen Tueller. 2017. "Health-Related Coping Behaviors and Mental Health in Military Personnel." *Military Medicine* 182 (3-4): e1620–e1627. https://academic.oup.com/milmed/article/182/3-4/e1620/4099460.

Murray, N., H. Sujan, E. R. Hirt, and M. Sujan. 1990. "The Influence of Mood on Categorization: A Cognitive Flexibility Interpretation." *Journal of Personality and Social Psychology* 59411–425.

n.d. "Papers of John F. Kennedy. Pre-Presidential Papers." *Senate Files. Series 12. Speeches and the Press. Box 899, Folder: "Gridiron Club, Washington, D.C., 15 March 1958"; David F. Powers Personal Papers. Series 09. John F. Kennedy Speeches File. Box 29, Folder: "Gridiron Club, Washington, DC, 15 March 1958".*

Peráčková, Janka, and Pavol Peráček. 2019. "Sport for the Subjective Dimensions of Quality of Life." In *Quality of Life—Biopsychosocial Perspectives*, edited by Floriana Irtelli. doi:10.5772/intechopen.88209.

Porter, Thomas W., and Daniel C. Smith. 2005. "Tactical Implementation and Murphy's Law: Factors Affecting the Severity of Problems." *Journal of Business Research* 1702–1711.

Saima, Sana, and Mohd Zohair. 2016. "Understanding Work-Life Balance with Respect to Medical Practitioners: A Conceptual Framework." *IUP Journal of Organizational Behavior*15(4):66–75.https://search.proquest.com/openview/5981b359bd6740eeaba147e387d18549/1?pq-origsite=gscholar&cbl=2029985.

Saxbe, Darby E., and Rena Repetti. 2010. "No Place Like Home: Home Tours Correlate With Daily Patterns of Mood and Cortisol." *Personality and Social Psychology Bulletin* 36 (1): 71–81. doi:10.1177/0146167209352864.

Shields, Grant S., Loren L. Toussaint, and George M. Slavich. 2016. "Stress-Related Changes in Personality: A Longitudinal Study of Perceived Stress and Trait Pessimism." *Journal Of Research In Personality* 6461–68.

Sife, Alfred, Edda Lwoga, and Camilius Sanga. 2007. "New Technologies for Teaching and Learning: Challenges for Higher Learning Institutions in Developing Countries." *International Journal of Education and Development Using ICT* 3 (2): 57–67. https://www.learntechlib.org/p/42360/.

Smith, Jack. 2019. "The Aristotelian Good Life and Virtue Theory." *International Journal of Business and Social Science* 10 (1): 6–12. doi:10.30845/ijbss.v10n1p2.

Tachibana, Koji. 2018. "Aristotle on Virtue and Friendship." *Proceedings of the XXIII World Congress of Philosophy.* 309–313. doi:10.5840/wcp232018221325.

Tomioka, Kimiko, Norio Kurumatani, and Hiroshi Hosoi. 2017. "Positive and Negative Influences of Social Participation on Physical and Mental Health among Community-Dwelling Elderly Aged 65–70 Years: A Cross-Sectional Study in Japan." *BMC Geriatrics* 17 (1): 111. doi:10.1186/s12877-017-0502-8.

World Health Organization. 1946. "Constitution." *World Health Organization.* July 22. Accessed 2019. https://www.who.int/about/who-we-are/constitution.

Yigitcanlar, Tan, Md. Kamruzzaman, Raziyeh Teimouri, Kenan Degirmenci, and Fatemeh Aghnaei Alanjagh. 2020. "Association Between Park Visits and Mental Health in a Developing Country Context: The Case of Tabriz, Iran." *Landscape and Urban Planning* 199: 103805. doi:10.1016/j.landurbplan.2020.103805.

Young, Mark A. 2005. *Negotiating the Good Life: Aristotle and the Civil Society.* 1st. London: Routledge. doi:10.4324/9781315248233.

The author Thomas J. Whitney was born in a small town in Central New York. Shortly after birth, his mother was injured in a car accident which left her paralyzed from the chest down permanently. It was right here where Thomas began to develop the "life is dark, so let it be" attitude. Growing up in a disabled family really taught him some hard values and perhaps overdeveloped his dark humor. Early in 2020, there was a life-changing event, and Thomas became an amputee himself. Life experience has led Thomas to a life of giving back through philanthropies. The main goal of life should be to help each other learn and grow.

Thomas, to this day, albeit disabled, still hopes to make this message known and in his first book, takes you along this journey. Thomas still lives in the same community and hopes to help people understand that there is comedic value all around us. Understanding that life is tough and we must learn to overcome its obstacles, he carries on. It is far too often that people get misguided by illusions of hope and misguided dreams. Thomas is determined to help society understand and overcome the obscurities of life.